Acclaim for Robin Lee Hatcher

"Robin Lee Hatcher weaves a romance with heart that grabs readers and won't let go. *Whenever You Come Around* pulled me in from the get-go. Charity Anderson, a beautiful, successful author with a deadline and a painful secret, runs into Buck Malone, a handsome, confirmed-bachelor, cowboy from her past, and he needs her help. I was captivated, and I guarantee you'll be rooting for them, too."

> — Sunni Jeffers, award-winning
> author of *Heaven's Strain*

"A heartwarming and engaging romance, *Whenever You Come Around* is a splendid read from start to finish!"

> — Tamera Alexander, *USA Today*
> bestselling author of *To Whisper
> Her Name* and *From a Distance*

"A handsome cowboy, horses, and a hurting heroine make for a winning combination in this newest poignant story by Robin Lee Hatcher. A gently paced but delightful ride, *Whenever You Come Around* will take readers on a journey of healing right along with the characters. Readers will feel at home in Kings Meadow and won't want to leave."

> — Jody Hedlund, bestselling author
> of *Love Unexpected*

"First loves find sweet second chances in King's Meadow. Heartwarming, romantic, and filled with hope and faith, this is Hatcher at her best!"

> — Lisa Wingate, National bestselling
> author of *The Story Keeper* and *The
> Prayer Box*

"In *Whenever You Come Around* Hatcher takes a look at the pain of secrets that kill the heart. But love indeed conquers all. Robin Lee Hatcher is the go-to classic romance author."

> — Rachel Hauck, Award winning,
> bestselling author of *The Wedding
> Dress*

"Robin Lee Hatcher has created an emotionally engaging romance, a story of healing and self forgiveness wrapped up in a package about small town life and a cowboy who lives a life honoring God. I want to live in King's Meadow."

— Sharon Dunn, author of *Cold Case Justice* and *Wilderness Target*

"*Whenever You Come Around* draws you into the beauty and history of the horse country of King's Meadow, Idaho. With every turn of the page, Robin Lee Hatcher woos readers with a love story of a modern-day cowboy and a city girl. Buck and Charity rescue each other from the lives they had planned—lives limited by fear. Instead, they discover their unexpected God-ordained happily ever after. A discerning writer, Hatcher handles Charity's past heartbreak with sensitivity and grace."

— Beth K. Vogt, author of *Somebody Like You*, one of *Publisher's Weekly's* Best Books of 2014

"*Whenever You Come Around* is one of Robin Lee Hatcher's pure-romance best, with a heroine waiting for total redemption and a strong hero of great worth. I find myself still smiling long after the final page has been read."

— Hannah Alexander, author of the Hallowed Halls series

"*Whenever You Come Around* is a slow dance of letting go of the past and its very real pain to step into the light of love. It's a story that will wrap around your soul with the hope that no past is so dark and haunted that it can't be forgiven and overcome. It's a love story filled with sweetness, tension, and slow fireworks. Bottom line, it was a romance I couldn't—and didn't want to—put down."

— Cara Putman, award-winning author of *Shadowed by Grace* and *Where Treetops Glisten*

"In *Love Without End*, Robin Lee Hatcher once again takes us to Kings Meadow, Idaho in a sweeping love story that captures the heart and soul of romance between two people who have every reason not to fall in love. With an interesting backstory interspersed among the contemporary chapters, and well-drawn, relatable secondary characters, Hatcher hits the mark with her warm and inviting love story."

— Martha Rogers, author of the series, Winds Across the Prairie and The Journey Homeward

"*Love Without End*, the first book in the new Kings Meadow Romance series, again intertwines two beautiful and heartfelt romances. One in the past and one in the future together make this a special read. I'm so glad Robin wrote a love story for Chet who suffered so much in *A Promise Kept* (January 2014). Kimberly, so wrong for him, becomes so right. Not your run of the mill cowboy romance—enriched with the deft writing and deep emotion."

— Lyn Cote, author of *Honor*, first in
the Quaker Bride series

"No one writes about the joys and challenges of family life better than Robin Lee Hatcher and she's at the top of her game with *Love Without End*. This beautiful and deeply moving story will capture your heart as it captured mine."

— Margaret Brownley, *NY Times*
bestselling author

"*Love Without End*, Book One in Robin Lee Hatcher's new Kings Meadow series, is a delight from start to finish. The author's skill at depicting the love and challenges of family has never been more evident as she deftly combines two love stories—past and present—to capture readers' hearts and lift their spirits."

— Marta Perry, author of
The Forgiven, Keepers of the
Promise, Book One

"I always expect excellence when I open a Robin Lee Hatcher novel. She never disappoints. The story here reminds me of a circle without end as Robin takes us through a modern day romance while looping one character through a WWII tale of love and loss and the resurrection of hope and purpose. *Love Without End* touched my heart and guided me to some wonderful truths of how God's love is a gift and a treasure."

— Donita K. Paul, bestselling author

"A beautiful, heart-touching story of God's amazing grace, and how He can restore and make new that which was lost."

— Francine Rivers, *New York Times*
bestselling author, regarding *A
Promise Kept*

Other Novels by Robin Lee Hatcher

Whenever You Come Around

A Kings Meadow Romance

Robin Lee Hatcher

THOMAS NELSON
Since 1798

NASHVILLE   MEXICO CITY   RIO DE JANEIRO

Published in Nashville, Tennessee, by Thomas Nelson. Thomas Nelson is a registered trademark of HarperCollins Christian Publishing, Inc.

Thomas Nelson titles may be purchased in bulk for educational, business, fund-raising, or sales promotional use. For information, please e-mail SpecialMarkets@ThomasNelson.com.

Publisher's Note: This novel is a work of fiction. Names, characters, places, and incidents are either products of the author's imagination or used fictitiously. All characters are fictional, and any similarity to people living or dead is purely coincidental.

Library of Congress Cataloging-in-Publication Data

Hatcher, Robin Lee.
  Whenever you come around / Robin Lee Hatcher.
     pages ; cm. — (A King's Meadow romance ; 2)
   Summary: "Just when Charity's wild imagination failed her, a flesh-and-blood hero walked into her life. Best-selling author Charity Anderson returns to her hometown of Kings Meadow to defeat a bad case of writer's block. She imagines she'll spend a lonely summer writing and then return to her home in Boise. She soon finds herself caring for Buck Malone, a wilderness guide — and the object of her unrequited teenage crush. But what else can she do? Her dog Cocoa caused the accident that left Buck with a broken ankle and wrist, taking him off the trail for weeks of prime tourist-season work. Buck and Charity have gone different ways since high school, and at first it seems they have little in common. Buck loves the simple, low-key life he's made for himself in the mountains of Idaho, and she's a woman accustomed to the faster, bustling pace of the city. But spending so much time together has Buck hoping to change her mind about staying in the small town she thought she'd left behind for good. It's a summer for discovering that young love is a spark not soon extinguished"— Provided by publisher.
  ISBN 978-1-4016-8769-4 (softcover)
 1. First loves—Fiction. 2. Man-woman relationships—Fiction. I. Title.
  PS3558.A73574W475 2015
  813'.54—dc23   2014044614

Printed in the United States of America

15 16 17 18 19 20 RRD 6 5 4 3 2

To Jerry, with love.

Official Web Site of Kings Meadow, Idaho

Kings Meadow welcomes you.

Tucked away in the mountains north of Boise, Idaho, Kings Meadow (population 2,893) is rich in history. The first white man to enter this valley was a miner named John Leonard. Having failed to find his fortune panning for gold, he chose to raise cattle, knowing that the men and women pouring into the Boise Basin in search of wealth needed to eat and would want his beef. The year was 1864. The Leonards have continued to ranch in this valley for the past 150+ years, raising beef cattle well into the twentieth century. Now the ranch is renowned for its champion quarter horses.

One of the local legends was a man by the name of Zeb McHenry who also came to Idaho Territory in the early days of the Boise Basin Gold Rush. Little is known about him after he left the area in 1865. However, it was McHenry who introduced this lush, green valley and the cattle raised by John Leonard to the miners in the Boise Basin.

Hikers and horseback riders can still see the remains of McHenry's cabin and sluice box.

In 1866, the town of Kings Meadow was founded on the southwest end of the valley. Folklore says the name "Kings" was chosen because of an unfinished chess game between John Leonard and Zeb McHenry.

Residents and visitors love the beauty of nature that surrounds the valley during the summer and winter. Pine-covered mountains rise to about 7,000 feet above sea level on all sides. Hot springs abound. The tranquil Gold Queen River winds its way from east to west; after leaving the valley, it merges with the South Fork of the Payette River, famous for its whitewater. Wildlife is abundant.

In Kings Meadow, horses can still be found tied up outside the local watering holes, and formal attire for weddings may include boots and cowboy hats.

Come and visit us. We'll make you feel at home.

Chapter 1

CHARITY ANDERSON PULLED INTO THE DRIVEWAY OF
her parents' home early on a Wednesday morning. The wood
shutters were closed over all the main-floor windows. Her
parents might as well have put up a sign: *Owners Away! Help
Yourselves!* Then again, this was Kings Meadow. Neighbors
looked out for neighbors and their property. It wasn't like in
the city where you could live next door to people for a decade
and not even know their names.

Taking a deep breath, she exited her automobile. Cocoa,
her brindle-colored dog—a Heinz 57 mixed breed with a
stocky body and short coat—jumped out right behind her
and began to sniff around.

"Your nose must think it's in heaven." Charity headed for
the front door. "Come on, girl. Let's check things out."

The calendar said June, but the cold, dreary interior of
the darkened house felt more like February. The first thing
Charity did was turn up the thermostat to get some heat

pumping into the rooms. The next was to open all of the shutters to let in the light.

"Well now, that helps. Doesn't seem quite as desolate, does it?"

She stopped a moment and looked around, realizing it was the first time she'd ever stayed here by herself. It would feel strange without either her parents or her older sister, Terri, for company. Their parents were on a three-month tour of Europe and the Mediterranean. "The trip of a lifetime," her mom had called it. "We're finally going." Her parents had scrimped and saved for the extended tour for the last thirty-five years.

As for Terri, she lived with her husband and daughter near Sun Valley, close to a three-hour drive from Kings Meadow. Charity didn't expect to see much of her over the summer.

"Well, I'm not in Kings Meadow for visiting, anyway," she said to Cocoa, who was exploring the house as if she'd never been in it before. "I guess you haven't been here often. Have you, girl?"

A desperate need for solitude and silence had brought Charity to Kings Meadow. Her Victorian-era home on the Boise River—the one she'd bought several years earlier because of its charm and interesting floor plan—had been flooded this spring when the river overflowed its banks. The water damage had been serious enough, but the cleanup had also revealed significant structural issues that would require months of remodeling work.

Maybe you shouldn't have bought the place without getting another inspection. Maybe you shouldn't make snap decisions all the time. Maybe if you'd follow Mom's advice every now and then . . .

"I'm trying," she whispered, "but it isn't easy."

Setting her jaw, she threw off her troubled thoughts and headed up the stairs. The second-floor bedroom she'd shared with her sister up until Terri got married—right out of high school—hadn't changed much. It still bore many of the traces of teenaged girls—possessions Terri and Charity hadn't wanted to take with them when they moved out, things their mother had been unable to get rid of.

She picked up a glass figurine from the nightstand and turned it over in the palm of her hand. She'd won the crystal horse at the fair the summer before her senior year. The whole family had been there that night—Mom and Dad; Terri and her husband, Rick, and their new baby; and Charity. She remembered the lights from the carnival rides, the loud music, the smells of hamburgers, grilled onions, and chorizos along Food Row, and the laughter. Lots and lots of laughter.

The pleasant memories made Charity smile as she unpacked her suitcases, placing some clothes in the old chest of drawers and hanging other items in the closet. There wasn't a lot of room in the latter. It had become a storage area for whatever size clothes her mother couldn't fit into at present.

When Charity's suitcases were emptied at last, she stowed them under her old bed. As she straightened, she looked out the window . . . and saw Buck Malone exit the house next door.

Buck Malone.

Her heart gave a crazy and unexpected flutter. She hadn't seen Buck in ages. Not even from a distance. But her old high school classmate—and secret heartthrob—was just as drop-dead gorgeous as he'd ever been. Perhaps more so. His shoulders were broader, and he looked taller too. *Was* he taller or was it a figment of her imagination?

Stop it, she mentally berated herself. It didn't matter. Buck was no one to her now. Just someone from her distant past. One of many someones from her distant past.

She watched him get into an old beater truck. The engine started, and in moments he'd pulled out of the driveway. Only after he was out of sight did she realize she'd begun to shake. Something dark and familiar lurked in her memory, and it took all of her resolve to block it out again. Weak in the knees, she sank onto the edge of the bed.

Breathe. Just breathe. It's all right. You're okay. You're safe.

Bit by bit, she willed her trembling hands to still, her heart to calm. These terrible feelings, these black thoughts and feared memories, were why she avoided coming home as much as possible. They were why she'd cut herself off from lifelong friends, why she'd erected barriers between herself and the people she loved. She hated the sense of being emotionally out of control. *Better to stay away from Kings Meadow than to feel this way.*

Only she didn't have a choice right now. Not really. Not with her house in complete disarray—hammers hammering, saws sawing, drills drilling for nine hours or more every day. Not with a book due all too soon at her publishers. Her parents' empty home had been the perfect and only logical answer to her dilemma.

She drew in another deep breath through her nose. *Better. Much better.* The shaking had stopped. Her pulse no longer raced. She could do this.

Rising from the bed, she saw Cocoa seated in the bedroom

doorway, watching her with a patient gaze. "Guess we'd better think about stocking the refrigerator so we don't go hungry. Let's go to the store."

Her dog knew what "Let's go" meant. Cocoa raced down the stairs and danced around impatiently until Charity caught up with her, purse slung over her shoulder. When Charity opened the door, the dog dashed outside and sniffed around the yard a bit before meeting her at the car.

Gazing fondly at the panting animal, Charity chuckled. "You're a silly girl, aren't you?" She leaned over and affectionately scrubbed behind the dog's ears. With a groan, Cocoa melted against her leg.

Charity's heart melted too. She loved this dog more than she'd thought possible. She'd rescued Cocoa from the shelter when she was an awkward-looking pup of about eight months old. Charity had been told the puppy was to be destroyed in three more days if no one adopted her. Maybe the girl at the shelter had known a soft touch when she saw one or maybe she'd spoken the truth. Whatever. Charity had left the shelter with Cocoa on a leash. She'd never been sorry for it either. The dog might not be beautiful in show terms—she was definitely not a purebred anything and part of her right ear had been torn off in a fight at the shelter—but she was smart as a whip and loved her mistress as much as Charity loved her. One-dog woman had met one-woman dog.

"Come on, then." She opened the car door and Cocoa jumped into the driver's seat, hopped over the console, and sat on the passenger side. Charity laughed again. The dog didn't care where they were going. She just liked to go.

Wouldn't things be simpler if we could all be like that?

The drive to the grocery store in Kings Meadow took less than ten minutes, even with a couple of stop signs between the Anderson home and the market. There was plenty of parking available in the small lot at this time of day. Out of habit she chose a spot farthest from the store entrance where her SUV was less likely to get dinged by other doors. Then she grabbed the leash and fastened it to Cocoa's collar.

"Come on, girl. We'll find you some shade."

Charity walked to the front of the store where she slid the leash over a post. "Cocoa, down. Stay." The dog obediently flopped down. "Good girl."

That taken care of, Charity stepped toward the automatic doors, which opened before her. The woman behind the checkout stand immediately looked in her direction. Her eyes widened.

"Charity Anderson. As I live and breathe. Is that you?"

"It's me, Mrs. Cook."

"When was the last time you came home, girl?"

"It's been awhile."

"Uh-huh." The other woman nodded vigorously, a smile breaking across her face. She looked Charity up and down.

This was one thing Charity didn't miss about small-town life: everybody being in everybody else's business. Never being able to go somewhere without being recognized. But there was no avoiding it, and she might as well tell Laura Cook what the woman wanted to hear. "You'll be seeing more of me for a while. I'm here for the summer."

"Is that right? Come to think of it, I guess I did hear that from someone. Something about your house getting torn apart. Those old houses are like that."

Nobody gets anything by you, Mrs. Cook. Charity yanked a shopping cart free and dropped her bag into it.

"We're all so proud of you, dear," the woman continued. "You know. The success of your books and all. Don't think I ever got to tell you that face-to-face. To think I knew you when you were a shy thing with braces on your teeth. And now you're famous."

"Hardly famous, Mrs. Cook. But I love what I do." *Most of the time.*

With a quick wave, she moved toward the first aisle, ending the conversation before she was tricked into sharing information she would prefer to keep to herself.

BUCK'S BROTHER, KEN, RAN HIS HAND OVER THE saddle Buck had finished making the day before. "Nice. Best one I've seen of yours."

"Thanks."

"Ever think of giving up being a guide and doing this year-round?"

"Nope." Buck shook his head. "I like what I do, just the way I do it."

"You'll never get rich."

Buck barked a laugh. "And you're gonna get rich as an educator?"

Ken tried to pull off an older-and-wiser brother glare, but it didn't work. In a moment he chuckled too. "You've got me there." He touched the saddle a second time. "Who's it for?"

"Kimberly Leonard. A gift from her husband."

"There's a city girl I never expected to stick around for long."

Buck glanced down at the leather bridle on the workbench. "I guess love'll do that to you. But I wouldn't know for sure. You're the one who's lucky in that department."

"No argument from me."

Buck meant it. Ken was lucky. No. More than that. Blessed. He and his wife, Sara, had fallen in love in high school, married while Ken was still in college, had three kids in quick succession, and now, ten years later, were expecting their fourth.

Buck, on the other hand, had never tried to find the "right one." Not that he hadn't known many nice women. Plenty of them. But he didn't have any desire to settle down. He'd lived enough years doing the responsible thing, taking care of others, paying off debt. He deserved to have fun. To be, as his mom called it, "footloose and fancy free." Nobody was going to change his mind about that. Not his brother and definitely not some female with marriage on her mind.

"You getting ready for a trip?" Ken asked, intruding on Buck's thoughts.

"Yeah. I leave next week. A dozen boys and two leaders from their church are packing in for a week to clear some trails."

Buck didn't merely like what he did as a wilderness guide. He loved it. And what wasn't to love? Spending most of the summer and early fall on horseback, riding through the beautiful Idaho backcountry, sleeping under the stars.

"They've got their own mounts," he continued, "and supposedly they're all good horsemen."

Not that it's ever perfect, he qualified to himself. Some of his clients weren't ready for the trips they went on, whether it was their riding skills or their inability to rough it or—worse yet—both. When that happened, a trip could be challenging. But even then, he loved what he did as an outfitter. It was a simple life. He made enough money to feed his horses and pay his low-interest mortgage. And in the winter he had his custom saddle work.

Changing the subject, he asked, "How's Sara?"

"Still tired." His brother's expression turned grim. "I'm worried, to tell you the truth. The doctor says she might have to go on bed rest until the baby's born. Not sure how we'll manage if that happens. The kids are already helping out as much as they can."

"I say it a lot, but if there's anything I can do, all you gotta do is ask."

"I know. Thanks, Buck. I appreciate it." Ken headed for the door. "Gotta run. Sara gave me a list of things I need to do before I go home."

"Tell her I'm praying for her."

"I'll do it."

After Ken left, Buck rose from the workbench and looked toward Antton Zubiar, the owner of the custom leather shop. "Thanks for letting me use your tools, Antton."

"Always welcome," the man answered with a wave of his gnarled hand.

Antton Zubiar had forgotten more about handcrafting the finest leather goods than Buck could ever hope to learn. Which was just one reason he liked hanging around the old Basque's cramped, dusty workshop.

He bid the man a good day, then got in his truck and drove to the Merc, where he parked a couple of spaces over from a silver Lexus. He'd seen the luxury SUV in the Anderson family's driveway when he'd left his house this morning. Had to be the same one. There weren't a whole lot of cars like that in these mountains.

Only one person would drive a Lexus and be parked at the Anderson house—Charity Anderson herself. He hadn't seen her in a long time. Years. But he'd seen her photo in the local newspaper a couple of times and heard about her plenty. A Kings Meadow High graduate publishing a series of bestselling novels before she turns thirty? That was big news around here. Folks were proud of her success. Especially her parents, who were now his next-door neighbors.

As if summoned by his thoughts, Charity came out of the market pushing a cart full of canvas shopping bags. At least he thought it was Charity. The photos in the newspaper hadn't done her justice. She'd been a bookish sort back in school. A little plump. Kind of a plain Jane, but nice. And very, very bright.

Nothing plump or plain about her now. Slender and shapely, she wore skinny jeans, a sky-blue fitted top, and high heels— heels that didn't belong anywhere in these mountains.

She turned to a dog that lay in the shade. With a quick motion, she freed the animal's leash from a concrete post. Then, leash in hand, she grabbed the handle of the shopping cart again and started toward her car. Halfway across the lot, she glanced up and saw Buck. She stopped, a strange expression crossing her face. Almost as if she found meeting up with him unpleasant or something.

"Hi, Buck." She smiled.

He must have imagined her first reaction. She sounded friendly enough now. "Hey, Charity. Is that really you? Haven't seen you in years. How are you?"

"I'm fine." She used the remote to open the back of her vehicle. "How about you?"

"Here. Let me get those for you." He strode over to help load the new-looking canvas bags full of groceries into the car.

"It's okay. You don't have to—"

"My mom would tan my hide if I didn't help a lady."

Charity took a step back, leaving him more room to work. He had all the bags loaded into the vehicle in a matter of moments. After closing the rear door, he turned toward her again. She stood with arms crossed over her chest, looking defensive. As if she didn't want to be near him. No sign of that fleeting smile. Maybe he hadn't been wrong about her reaction.

Hoping to thaw the chill between them, he said, "I like your dog."

Her expression didn't change. Not a bit. "Thanks."

Stubborn, isn't she? Well, he could be stubborn too. "How's the trip for your folks so far? Are they having a great time?"

At last there came a glimmer of a smile again. "Yes. I had an e-mail from them last night." She drew a deep breath, as if steeling herself to continue the conversation. "They're still getting over the jet lag but are enjoying the sites of London before they head to Paris."

"Glad to hear it. Are you up here for long?"

She didn't answer at once. "For the summer, actually."

"The summer? I guess that means I'll see more of you

then, now that we're neighbors. You knew I bought the place next door to your parents, right?"

"Yes, I knew. But I don't plan to be out and about much. I'll be writing most of the time. And listen, I really must get back to the house. I've got lots to do."

Buck couldn't remember the last time he'd gotten the brush-off from a woman. It irritated him more than it should, and now he was the one who wanted to leave. "Sure. Don't want to keep you. I'll take the cart in. That's where I was headed anyway."

At least going inside the store was what he'd intended. But things quickly went awry. Charity started to turn. Then she gave a little squeal of surprise and swayed to the side, looking as if she might topple over. Buck shoved the cart away and grabbed for her, but before he took hold, something caught him from the behind his knees, causing them to buckle. Next, his legs were yanked out from under him. He tried to break his fall with his hand. Despite it, he hit the ground hard.

For one blessed moment he felt nothing but surprise. Then the pain shot through him. A white-hot haze of agony. So bad he couldn't be sure where in his body it came from. Not good. He closed his eyes, sweat instantly beading his forehead.

"Buck. Oh, I'm sorry." Charity's voice seemed far away. "Cocoa, sit. *Sit!*"

Buck groaned and tried to push himself up from the black-top. The pain became more specific as his right arm crumpled beneath him.

Charity knelt beside him. "Are you okay?"

"I don't think so," he answered, breathing hard. "What happened?"

"The leash. Cocoa. Oh, I'm so sorry."

Someone called Charity's name.

"We need the EMTs, Mrs. Cook," she shouted back, looking toward the store entrance.

At least Buck thought the store was in that direction. The world felt upside down and inside out right now, so he couldn't be sure of anything.

"I think you've broken your wrist. It's . . . it's turned kind of . . . funny. Try to hold still."

Better not to look, he thought, closing his eyes again. "I must've twisted my ankle too." He spoke through clenched teeth. "It's like it's on fire."

"The EMTs will be here soon." She took his left hand in hers and held on firmly.

Buck didn't doubt his wrist was broken. His ankle, too, more than likely. He knew what it felt like—between horses and sports, he'd been busted up before.

But never at the start of the tourist season.

His heart sank. If he had a broken bone or two, he was in trouble. He'd have to find another outfitter to fill in for him on the trips he'd booked for the next few weeks. Finding somebody good on such short notice wouldn't be easy.

Nothing about this accident is going to help my bottom line.

Crazy, the way those concerns shot through his head even as he made an effort to draw breath and ignore the pain.

Chapter 2

Kings Meadow had a small medical clinic that served the community as a hospital for noncritical cases. That was where the EMTs took Buck after stabilizing his wrist and ankle. Charity followed the ambulance from the market to the clinic and then sat in the waiting area, feeling guilty.

Why, why, why, did this have to happen? As if I didn't have enough to deal with.

She'd felt the spiked heel of her shoe drop into a crack in the pavement of the store's parking lot. If she hadn't cried out in surprise, afraid she would fall . . . If Buck hadn't shoved the shopping cart and grabbed for her . . . If none of those things had happened, maybe Cocoa wouldn't have been startled and wouldn't have darted behind him, the leash catching him at the knees. Cocoa was a medium-sized dog, but she was solid muscle from head to toe. She was strong enough to take down a man double Buck's size.

The door to the clinic swung open, and Ken Malone

strode into view, bright sunlight at his back. Unlike Buck, Charity had seen Ken on a few of her rare visits home. He was the principal at the high school—had been for about five years—and his wife, Sara, was a close friend of Terri's.

Ken looked around. When he saw Charity, he walked in her direction rather than going to the reception desk. "Are you here with Buck?"

She nodded. "I'm pretty sure he broke some bones."

"What happened?"

"He fell in the parking lot of the Merc."

Ken's eyebrows arched. "Fell?"

"My dog knocked him off his feet," she clarified with great reluctance.

Buck's brother might have had something more to say to that, but he was interrupted by the appearance of the doctor. Charity didn't know the young-looking man in the white coat and assumed he was the new physician her mother had told her about. Gray something or something Gray. He'd come to Kings Meadow about eight months ago, if she remembered right.

"I'm Dr. Frederick."

That was it. Dr. Gray Frederick.

"Are you Mr. Malone's brother?" the doctor continued, looking at Ken.

"Yes. How is he?"

"He's broken bones in his right wrist and ankle. Surgery isn't necessary, but he won't be very mobile for the next six to eight weeks. He can't put weight on his ankle, and with the broken wrist, crutches won't be of much use to him. He's going to need help, especially at first. He tells me he lives alone."

"Yes, he does."

"Can you stay with him for a few days?"

"Is it that serious?"

"It would be better if he wasn't alone right at first."

Ken ran the fingers of one hand through his hair. "I can help out, but I can't be with him 24/7. My wife's pregnant and having a difficult time. I need to be nearby as much as possible for her and our three kids."

The doctor's eyes shifted to Charity. She supposed he wondered if she was the pregnant sister-in-law. Which she obviously wasn't. But with the doctor's gaze on her, her guilt over the incident surged back to life. "I'm staying next door to him for the summer. I . . . I can look in on him." Oh, how difficult it was to say those words. She'd come here to work, not to take care of Buck Malone. Even if it was her fault he needed help.

Ken said, "We can count on his friends to pitch in too."

"Good. Good." The doctor nodded. "Then I'll get back to my patient. You'll have a bit of a wait before he's ready to go home."

"No problem, Dr. Frederick." After the doctor walked away, Ken sat on the chair next to Charity. "This came at a bad time for everybody."

"I . . . I'm sorry to hear about Sara having a rough go of it."

"Thanks. The good part is that our kids are at an age where they can look after themselves for the most part. Our youngest, Jake, is ten."

"Ten? Already?" For a moment she remembered what might have been.

Ten years.

"Yeah. Time goes by fast."

Sometimes, maybe. Sometimes it crawls by.

She mentally slapped herself. *Stop it!* She hated the way her thoughts kept twisting, the feeling of being stuck in the past. Hated it. Even hated herself because of it. *Why can't I just move on?* It wasn't as if she hadn't tried.

"Hey, listen," Ken said, breaking into her thoughts. "Would it really be all right for you to check in on Buck every now and then?"

She drew in a long, slow breath, longing to say, *No, come to think of it. It isn't all right.*

Ken didn't seem to notice. "I know he'll get help from friends. But, well, it would give me peace of mind to know you're right there next door and willing and able to help if you're needed."

What choice did she have? The accident was her fault, plain and simple. Who better to help him? Besides, if she didn't give aid to a neighbor and her mom heard about it, there'd be you-know-what to pay.

She rose from the waiting area chair. "Give me a call when you've brought Buck home." Fishing for a business card, she handed it to Ken. "When the breeze is right, the signal is strong enough for you to catch me on my mobile phone. Otherwise call my parents' house line."

"I'll do it." He wiggled the card. "See you in a while."

MEDICATION HELPED DULL THE PAIN IN BUCK'S body, but it didn't help much with the worry circling in his head. He wouldn't be able to walk for weeks. He was right-handed but had no use of his right wrist. He would have to contact his clients and either cancel their trips or find new guides for them. Either way, he'd lose important income and rack up debt at the same time. His high-deductible insurance would help cover some of the medical expenses but not much. Not enough. And who would feed and water his animals twice a day? Another favor to ask of someone. Not easy for a guy with an independent spirit.

"I'll come over as often as I can," his brother said as he drove toward Buck's home. "Friends will pitch in. You know that already. Probably won't have to worry about food the entire time you're laid up. I bet there'll be at least two casseroles delivered by the ladies of Kings Meadow before dinner tonight."

Buck closed his eyes. Food didn't sound too good to him. The drugs were making him dizzy and queasy. It was a rare thing for him to take even an over-the-counter pain reliever, let alone anything as strong as what they'd given him at the clinic, and he was definitely feeling it.

"And Charity offered to look in on you since she's staying right next door."

Buck pictured blue eyes and dark-blond hair and high heels, but he couldn't pull up the entire face. His head was stuffed with cotton. Ken asked a question, but Buck couldn't make sense of his brother's words . . .

The next thing he knew, Ken's vehicle was parked close to Buck's back door and his brother stood at the passenger's side door, ready to help him out.

"Think we can manage this?" Ken asked.

Buck blinked a few times. "Yeah, I think so."

He twisted slowly on the seat and set his good foot on the ground. Ken reached in, putting his hands beneath Buck's arms, and heaved him up and out of the car. He then stuck a crutch under Buck's left armpit.

Buck swayed unsteadily. "I think my good leg's made of rubber."

"Not sure I can carry you, bro, but I'll try if I need to."

"No. I can do this. Just give me a second. The meds they gave me aren't playing nice with my equilibrium."

Ken held Buck steady until he was ready to try hopping on one foot toward the door, using the crutch on his left side and his brother on his right. It took awhile, but eventually they made it into the house. They stopped in the living room and Buck dropped onto the sofa.

I'm as winded as an old man.

Ken went to the bedroom, returning with pillows to prop up Buck's leg. "What else can I get you? Need help into the bathroom?"

"Just some water, I think."

"And the telephone. You're going to have to call for help when nobody's here with you." Ken walked to the kitchen as he spoke, raising his voice a little while in the other room. "No trying to get around yourself. No weight on that ankle. You've got to follow doctor's orders or you'll pay for it later."

Buck groaned. Having to ask for help didn't come easily for him. He was the one used to helping others, not being helped.

I can do for myself.

Ken returned with a bottle of water and the telephone. "Don't do anything stupid, Buck, while you're here alone."

"I won't." He closed his eyes. "All I want to do is sleep right now. Just let me go to sleep."

His brother might have spoken again, but Buck heard nothing more.

* * *

When Buck managed to resurface, he discovered Charity seated in a chair on the opposite side of the living room, tapping her fingers on the keyboard of her laptop. Ken must have left. But how long ago? He shifted his position on the couch. The movement drew Charity's gaze from the laptop screen.

"Hey," he said, his voice gruff in his ears. "What're you doing here?"

If his question insulted her, she didn't show it.

"Sorry. That was rude." He pushed himself to a sitting position. The room swayed but then righted itself again. "Ken asked you to look after me, didn't he?"

"Yes." She nodded.

Despite her guarded expression and his muddled brain, he guessed the reason she was there. "You don't have to feel guilty, Charity. It was an accident."

"I know."

"Is your dog okay? I didn't fall on him, did I?"

This, at last, softened her expression. "No, you didn't fall on *her*. Cocoa's fine."

"That's a relief." He held out his right arm and stared at his cast. Beneath it, he felt a dull throb of pain. Nothing unbearable, but definitely there. He swung his right leg around to rest on the coffee table. The pain was worse in his ankle.

"Can I get you anything?" Charity set her laptop on an end table and rose to her feet.

Bare feet, Buck noticed, with bright-pink polish on her nails. For some reason that made him want to grin.

"Would you like something to eat? There are a couple of casseroles in the fridge. Your pastor's wife brought them over."

Ken was right on that one.

"Not yet. Not feeling very hungry. But my horses will be."

"Your brother said they're taken care of and you aren't to worry about them."

Buck reached for the bottle of water on the coffee table, held it between his knees while he removed the cap with his left hand, and then took several long swallows. It helped the scratchiness of his throat. Only, the less he drank, the less often he would need to use the bathroom, so that was something he ought to consider. And how was he going to get there when the time came? It wasn't like he wanted to ask Charity—a never-married female and no relation—to help get him there. Besides, she was a slip of a thing. He doubted she could lift anything heavier than an unabridged dictionary.

As if reading his thoughts, she walked to the corner of the room nearest the front door. "Mayor Abbott was in Boise on business when he learned about your accident, and he rented this for you from a medical supply store down in the valley. He delivered it a bit ago and said you need to call the store with your insurance information." She rolled a three-wheeled scooter toward the sofa. "You put your right knee on this padded rest and hold on to the handlebars. With that cast on your hand and arm, it won't be easy, but it'll be better than a wheelchair, and Ken said you can't do crutches. Ready to try it out?"

He answered with a slight shake of his head.

"Tom Butler volunteered to stay with you at night for as long as you need him." She checked her wristwatch. "He ought to be here soon."

"I don't think I'll need him to stay."

"The doctor thought it would be a good idea until you've mastered the scooter. At least one night." She pointed at his cast. "Because you can't use your wrist. That's going to make things lots harder than you think, he said."

Buck was about to insist more strenuously that he didn't need anybody to look after him. Instead, he paused, considering the situation. Actually, it might be nice to have Charity around. He was laid up for weeks. He might as well enjoy the time off in the company of a pretty woman. Besides, she intrigued him. "Small-town girl makes good" and all that. Not to mention how standoffish she had been toward him. She presented something of a challenge, and that might make the coming weeks of idleness less tedious and boring.

"All right," he said, shrugging in a show of surrender. "I give up. If the doctor thinks I need help, I'll listen to him. I don't want to make the injuries any worse than they are now."

He grinned and Charity, as though sensing his thoughts, eyed him warily. He schooled his features to innocence.

Oh yeah, this was going to be fun.

Chapter 3

EARLY THE NEXT MORNING, CHARITY STOOD ON THE front stoop, sipping her first cup of coffee, while Cocoa sniffed in the flowerbeds.

She hadn't slept well. She'd lain awake for several hours, heard every small creak and groan of the older home. And once she had fallen asleep, unpleasant dreams had caused more tossing and turning. Coming home always did that to her. She didn't want to dwell on why.

The closing of a car door drew her attention to her neighbor's house. She watched Tom Butler climb behind the wheel of a sedan, but he didn't look her way as he started the engine. Perhaps just as well, considering she was still in her pajamas on this brisk morning.

"Come on, Cocoa. Inside."

In the kitchen, she drank the last of the coffee in her mug. She didn't need to remind herself that she had to make significant progress on her book before she did her neighborly duty. The deadline was always in the forefront of her thoughts.

Why did he have to go and break bones in that stupid fall? Why did I have to get roped into taking care of him?

Guilt immediately stabbed her. Buck hadn't broken those bones by himself. It had taken help from her and Cocoa to accomplish it.

If only—

She cut the thought off in an instant. Those were two very dangerous words. Thinking *if only* was as dangerous as wondering *what if.* The first meant she was dwelling in the past and revisiting all of her mistakes. The second—although important in her job as a writer—meant she was worrying about the future. Both were a waste of emotions and energy. Both were something she had done far too much of over the years.

Help me, Lord, not to do that.

She sighed. Her belief in answered prayer was still a fragile thing. She'd turned her back on faith in God while in college and had done her best to ignore any suggestion—from her parents or her sister or anyone else—that she needed Jesus in her life. Up until about a year ago. That was when, in a moment of despair, she'd taken a few steps back in God's direction. In the months since, He'd restored her faith, not in one amazing moment, but in a thousand little ways.

Another lengthy restoration project. Isn't it, Lord?

She set the empty mug beside the coffeemaker and headed for the stairs, certain she would feel better once she was showered and dressed. And she was right. The spray of water washed away the remnants of her bad dreams and, more important, those shadowy memories that plagued her the most in Kings Meadow.

Sadly, the shower didn't do a thing for her creativity. She sat down at her desk, fingers on the keyboard, waiting for a flow of ideas. They didn't come.

"The muse has left the building." She groaned, letting her chin fall to her chest.

She had a secret fear: that she would never write anything as good as the Lancer series that had launched her writing career. Or could she even call it a career? Perhaps all she had in her was that single plotline told over the course of three books. Her *only* three books.

When she'd written her novels, she hadn't thought about trying to sell them to a publisher, as crazy as that sounded. She'd been wrapped up in the joy of storytelling, and that had been enough. At first. But then, with Terri nudging her—her sister was always nudging her about something—Charity had queried some agents. Before she'd known it, she had literary representation, followed soon by a publishing contract.

Everything seemed so perfect then.

It wasn't as if she'd written the next *Hunger Games*. Her series wasn't *that* popular. But it was popular enough. She'd been able to quit her day job and to buy a new car and her adorable old house on the river. She'd bought herself a stylish new wardrobe too. One that said, "Confident. Self-assured. Going places." Things she'd never thought would be true of her. She'd begun to dream new dreams for the future. Perhaps even a future that included love and marriage.

That's what she'd thought . . . for a little while.

Man plans and God laughs. So said a Yiddish proverb. It felt true to Charity.

Late the previous year, her publishing house had changed hands and direction. They would no longer be publishing young adult books, they'd told her. Despite the success of the Lancer series, they wanted Charity's next contracted novel to be for adults. A *romance* for adults. Romance? What did she know about romance? She'd spent a lot of years purposefully avoiding it.

She hadn't yet wrapped her head around the idea of writing a romantic novel when she'd learned the publisher had laid off her beloved editor, the one person she'd trusted more than anyone else in the business. How could she write an entirely different kind of book without her editor? It was unfair, unreasonable.

And then the other shoe had dropped—right on her head, it felt like. With no warning, her agent had closed his agency. Although he'd given Charity a few recommendations, she hadn't found another agent who seemed a good match, leaving her without representation or guidance up to now.

Cut adrift. She sighed.

The house phone rang, and Charity was glad for the interruption. "Hello?"

"Hey, Pipsqueak."

She smiled at the sound of her sister's voice. "Hey, Toot-sweet."

"How's it going? Are you writing already?"

"A little. But I've been distracted since getting here."

"By what?"

She hesitated a moment, then launched into the story

about Buck, from the time she'd seen him in the parking lot through the accident and right up until she'd seen Tom Butler leaving Buck's house this morning.

"Poor Buck," Terri said when Charity finally fell silent. "Not the kind of luck he needs. He's a good guy. Mom and Dad think the world of him. I'm glad you're helping out. Only fair. Your dog. Your fault."

As if she needed *that* reminder.

Terri took pity on her and changed the subject. They chatted for a short while about their parents, about Rick's job, and finally about Terri's family's vacation plans for later in the summer. Then Terri sighed. "I'm gonna have to run, sis. Frankie needs help studying for her finals. I just hope she never finds out she's smarter than her mom or I'm doomed."

Charity laughed. "Maybe her aunt will tell her."

"Don't you dare. But you can tell Buck I hope his recovery is swift and complete."

"Sure. I'll do it."

"And, Pipsqueak? Maybe you need to forget about that book for a little while and try to enjoy Kings Meadow again. You need to remember all the reasons it was so great to grow up there."

And just like that, Charity's mood darkened. *Enjoy Kings Meadow.* She didn't think that would ever be possible, but she could never tell her family why. It was her secret. She meant to take it to her grave.

"I love you, sis," Terri said. "Take care."

"You too." Charity waited until the line went silent before dropping the handset into its cradle. It was quite a few moments until she was able to shake herself free of memories and move on about her day.

BUCK WOULDN'T ADMIT IT TO ANOTHER SOUL, BUT he could see why the doctor thought he should have someone around every now and again. If he only had a broken ankle, the scooter would have made life a breeze. Or, for that matter, he would have been fine with crutches. Amazing how a little thing like a broken wrist could make everything else so complicated. Tom had offered to fix breakfast before he left, but Buck hadn't been hungry then. Now he was half starved but unable to get a casserole out of the refrigerator or even the tin off the top of a can of peaches. Frustration boiled up inside of him, and that was when he heard the knock at the front door.

"Come in!" he shouted, sounding as grumpy as he felt.

The door opened enough to let a head peek through. "Buck?"

"It's okay, Charity. It's safe to enter."

She looked toward the kitchen as she pushed the door open wide and stepped in. "Are you all right?"

"Not really. I'm hungry. *This*"—he held up his right arm—"is a royal pain in the neck."

She had the audacity to grin, although the expression didn't hang around her face for long.

He couldn't make up his mind if he wanted to kick her out or try to laugh with her. Both, he decided. Equally.

"I should have checked on you earlier," she said, walking into the kitchen. "I assumed you'd had breakfast already. What would you like to eat?"

"Cold cereal will be fine."

"Cardboard nutrition." She pointed at him. "You need a healthy diet to speed your recovery."

She sure was cute, wagging that finger in his direction. His bad mood began to dissipate.

"How about an omelet? With diced ham, cheese, and some sautéed mushrooms. I've got all the fixings in your fridge. I made sure of that yesterday."

"Sure," he answered. "An omelet will be fine."

"Great. I'll have it ready in no time." She motioned for him to move.

It was his turn to chuckle. "Bossy, aren't you?"

"Sorry. I'm used to being in charge. You know, because I live alone."

"I hear you." Holding on to the handlebar of the scooter with his left hand, he rolled across the small kitchen to the table. Trying not to look completely uncoordinated, he shifted off the scooter and plopped onto a chair.

With swift efficiency, Charity removed food items from the refrigerator. Under his direction, she found the chopping board, mixing bowl, utensils, and the skillet. Buck felt proud of himself for having everything she needed. The truth was he wasn't a great cook. He liked to barbecue, but he didn't spend much time in the kitchen.

"What made you decide to buy this place?" Charity asked as she began beating the eggs in the bowl.

"The twenty acres that went with it."

She glanced over at him, a question in her eyes.

"I don't need much when it comes to a house." He shrugged. "This one's big enough. A bedroom for me and one to spare should I ever have a guest. It's in decent shape for a house built in the forties. The last owner put on a new roof about eight years ago. There's a good stable for my horses and a couple of other outbuildings. There's even a small insulated workshop that I plan to use in the off-season."

"Use for what?" She returned her attention to the breakfast preparations.

Buck liked the sway of her hair against the back of her pink T-shirt. He'd always been a sucker for blondes with long, straight hair. Had she worn her hair that way in high school? He didn't think so.

She glanced at him again.

Oh. Yeah. Her question. "I make custom saddles. It's not my main source of income, but I enjoy it. I guess you could call it a hobby."

"Custom saddles aren't cheap."

"No." He shrugged again. "Guess you're right. It's more than a hobby. Helped get me the down payment on this place."

Charity stopped asking questions at that point. Soon the sounds, followed by the delicious odors, of food cooking in a hot skillet filled the kitchen. Again, Buck was content to watch her as she worked. It was easy to see she enjoyed what she was doing. He wouldn't have been surprised to hear her humming, the way her mother did when the Andersons had him over for dinner.

It wasn't long before she set a plate of the promised omelet on the table before him. "Orange juice? Or coffee?" she asked.

"OJ. Thanks."

He half expected her to start washing dishes right away,

but instead, she poured herself a cup of coffee and sat opposite him at the table. It pleased him—perhaps more than it should—that today she didn't seem to want to get away from him as quickly as possible.

He took his first bite of the omelet. Closed his eyes and moaned in pleasure. "Wow. Lots better than cereal."

She smiled, then sipped her coffee as he polished off the eggs in short order.

"Guess I proved how hungry I was." He set down the fork and leaned back in his chair before draining the glass of orange juice. "Bet you learned to cook like that from your mom."

She nodded in silence.

"Your folks've had me over for supper a few times since I moved in. Taking pity on the bachelor next door, I think. Anyway, your mom's a magician in the kitchen."

Charity laughed. It was a pretty sound. One he wouldn't mind hearing more of.

"Have you told Mom that?" she asked. "Nothing would make her happier than to hear those words. Preparing delicious food is one of her love languages, and Dad's expanding waistline is a consequence of all that devotion from the kitchen."

"I think she probably guessed what I thought by the way I cleaned my plate. If she keeps having me over, I'll be like your dad." He patted his stomach for emphasis, then eyed her thoughtfully. "So tell me something, Charity," he drawled.

Her eyebrows arched in question. "What's that?"

"From what I can tell, you almost never make it home to see your parents, and you only live in Boise. An hour away is all, more or less. And now, when they're gone, you come for the summer. What gives?"

He knew he'd made a mistake before the question left his lips. An instantaneous chill emanated from the other end of the table. Cold enough to form icicles on his day-old whiskers. Or just about. Without answering, Charity rose from her chair and cleared the dirty plate and juice glass from in front of him. Her gaze avoided his.

"Hey, I'm sorry, Charity. It's none of my business. It's just, I like your parents and I know they—"

"You're right. It's none of your business." She ran hot water into the sink and began washing the dishes.

Annoyed with her response, Buck remained at the table for a few minutes. She might be the prickliest female he'd ever come in contact with. Okay, so maybe he shouldn't have asked about her parents, but she didn't have to act like the question was a criminal offense either.

Don't think you've scared me off yet, Miss Anderson. I'll figure out what makes you tick. You'll see.

When she didn't turn or even look over her shoulder, he knew he was being ignored. Must be time to make himself scarce and let her calm down. He managed to rise and get his knee on the scooter without tipping over chair or table.

CHARITY LISTENED AS THE WHEELS ROLLED ACROSS the hardwood floor. Once she knew Buck was out of the kitchen, she released a slow breath.

Who does he think he is?

She stopped, bowed her head, and closed her eyes. Nobody had to remind her that her parents were hurt by the distance she kept between them. And since she'd steadfastly refused to tell them why she stayed away from Kings Meadow, they weren't ever going to understand.

I should have rented an apartment in Boise for the summer. I shouldn't have come up here. I thought I could handle it. Maybe I can't.

Drawing one more steadying breath, she finished the last of the cleanup, dried her hands on a dish towel, and then headed for the living room. Eyes averted, she said, "I need to get back to work."

She felt Buck studying her. "Hey, Charity. I really am sorry. Didn't mean to offend you or interfere. Forgive me?"

"Yes. It's all right." She reached for the doorknob. "I'll check in on you later, but call if you need anything before that."

"Sure."

She opened the door and escaped into the fresh morning air.

Chapter 4

"You almost never make it home to see your parents." The words echoed in Charity's memory for the next few hours. *"What gives?"*

When she couldn't turn off Buck's voice in her head—or the ache in her heart that it caused—she decided to take a drive, hoping to outrun the feelings churning inside of her. She made her way to the two-lane highway and drove east. Cocoa rode shotgun, her head out the window and tongue flapping in the wind.

"You almost never make it home to see your parents."

"I know," she whispered. "I know."

She loved her mom and dad. It wasn't their fault she'd stayed away all of these years. She was lucky they chose to come visit her as frequently as they did. Of course, they wondered why it had to be that way, but she'd never been able to tell them. Would never be able to tell them. She knew she couldn't. She'd tried many times.

He's gone from Kings Meadow now. You don't have to be afraid of seeing him. It's over. The past is done with.

"Only it isn't done," she said aloud.

The tears came, swift and blinding. She applied the brakes and pulled off to the side of the road before cutting the engine.

How could it still hurt this much after a decade? Ten years. She wasn't that stupid, naïve girl any longer. Why couldn't she pull herself up by her bootstraps, as her grandpa used to say, and get on with it? She'd tried. Heaven knew she'd tried. Again and again and again.

Tried plenty of the wrong things too.

She swiped at the tears on her cheeks.

"Maybe if I went there . . ."

Her heart began to hammer, her breath coming in shallow pants. Should she do it? Could she? She glanced over at Cocoa. The dog watched her with what seemed a compassionate, understanding gaze.

"If only you could understand," Charity whispered as she reached out to stroke Cocoa's head.

Odd, the way the action of petting her dog gave her the courage to start the car and pull back onto the highway. After two miles she turned left onto a connecting road. A few more miles and she turned right again.

The old Riverton place was located on a hillside, surrounded by forest, with tall wrought-iron fences and brick posts encircling the mansion and entire twenty-five-acre estate. It had belonged to Sinclair Riverton, a powerful and wealthy businessman who had moved with his wife to Kings Meadow in the late seventies. Two years after giving birth to their son, Jon, his wife had died. Sinclair—as well as the nanny, maids, butler, and cook—had raised his son to be a Riverton through and through. Which meant ruthless, heartless, and ambitious. That was exactly what Jon Riverton had become.

The front gates of the estate came into view. She drove up to them and stopped. It didn't matter if she parked there. The place was deserted these days. A large sign—at least six feet wide—hung on the fence to the right, red letters proclaiming the property for sale. Charity got out of the car, Cocoa on her heels. When she reached the gatehouse, she looked up the drive and caught a glimpse of the house.

Old Mr. Riverton must be rolling over in his grave.

Shifting, she put a hand against the walk-through gate and, unexpectedly, it swung open. A memory of that same gate, open on a moonless night, assailed her. She fell back against the side of the gatehouse, sweat beading on her forehead. Fear lay like lead in her stomach.

"Shh, Charity. You gotta be quiet."

Jon's hot, alcohol-laced breath seemed to brush against her cheek again, as it had done that night.

"Shh, Charity," Jon whispered. "You gotta be quiet. We don't want to wake up the help. The old man doesn't like me to have friends over when he's away."

The night was as black as ink, but up the hillside, lights from the house beckoned to them.

"Not a sound until I tell you it's okay," he said, his mouth right next to her ear.

She swayed unsteadily.

He caught her with hands on her shoulders. "Come on. Let's get you inside. It's getting cold out here."

Charity wasn't cold. Not even a little bit. The margaritas—she couldn't remember how many—had made certain of that. All the same, she was glad when he put his arm around her shoulders and held her close as they walked up the curved driveway. As the Riverton mansion came fully into view, golden light spilling from windows here and there, she released a soft gasp. Her only glimpses of this house had been from the road. Never in her life had she imagined she would be here with Jon Riverton himself.

She wasn't even sure how it had happened. He'd never noticed her back in high school. Not very many kids had, boys or girls. She'd been a nobody. An introvert in the extreme. Invisible.

But Charity had changed during her first two years at Boise State. She'd grown up, lost weight, learned to pretend to be confident even when she didn't feel it. She liked to party because it forced her to get outside, to be with others, to meet guys. She liked to drink a little more than she should, but not as much as many of her fellow students.

Tonight, at one of those college parties where the liquor never seemed to run out, Jon Riverton had come over to introduce himself to her. Not that he'd known who she was at first. Not until she told him who her parents were and where they lived. After about an hour—and a couple more drinks—Jon had suggested they leave the party, and she'd agreed to go with him. In the car, when he'd asked if she would like to see his home, she'd said yes. What girl wouldn't? Anyone in Kings Meadow would have answered the same. Any girl at BSU would have too. This was Sinclair Riverton's son who'd invited her. Of course she wanted to go.

Jon put an index finger to his lips as he opened a side entrance. And he didn't turn on the lights after closing the door. Instead, holding her hand and keeping her close behind him, he led the way through the dark room, down a long hallway, up a staircase, and into another room. Finally, a light came on. Charity blinked. Although not bright, the bulb in the bedside lamp almost blinded her. She held up a hand to shield her eyes.

"Welcome to my home." Jon tugged her farther into the room . . . and closer to the bed.

A tingle of fear ran down her spine.

His hands cupped her face. "Can't believe we never met before tonight."

I wasn't the kind of girl you noticed.

"You're so beautiful." He kissed her.

She'd been kissed before. Not in high school, but she'd had a few boyfriends since moving to Boise to attend the university. Nobody serious, but serious enough that kissing had been involved.

This was different somehow.

She drew back as far as he would allow. "Aren't you . . . aren't you going to show me the rest of the house?"

"Not right now, baby. Right now there's something else I want to show you."

Buck looked out the bedroom window, watching as Chet Leonard doled out feed to the six horses in the pasture.

As if he doesn't have enough to do at his own place. He shouldn't have to do for me too.

Buck had looked out for himself—and his family, much of the time—since he was eighteen. That was the summer his dad had been diagnosed with stage 4 cancer. In the months and years to come, Buck had learned how to be the dependable one, the capable one, the fearless one. He'd been the strong back to help his dad from the bedroom to the bathroom, from the car to the doctor's office. He'd been the shoulder for his mom to cry on when she lost hope. He'd been the one who made tough decisions when neither of his parents had been able to make any for themselves. Treatment. Hospice care. Burial or cremation. Mounting medical bills. Ken's college tuition. Selling the home he'd grown up in. Helping his widowed mom move to Arizona. Giving up for good on the dreams he'd had for his future.

He closed his eyes, trying to shut out the bad memories. He'd survived. He'd made a new and different life for himself. One he was content with. Dwelling in the past was a pointless exercise. He'd learned that a long time ago.

When he opened his eyes, he saw Chet striding toward the house. He turned the scooter around and rolled it toward the kitchen. He was getting better at steering it with only his left hand. He wouldn't win any races, but he wasn't running into the walls either. Well, he'd only done it once today.

Chet stopped at the back door and looked in through the screen. "You sure there's nothing else I can do for you?"

"No. Not a thing. You've done enough."

"Glad to help."

"Come on in, if you've got the time."

Chet pulled open the screen door. "I've got time."

Buck knew better. A rancher never had enough time. But Chet was the sort of man who put others first. Just one reason folks in Kings Meadow respected him.

"It's getting close to suppertime. Want me to get you something to eat?"

Before Buck could answer, his stomach growled. Both men laughed at the sound.

"I guess I could eat something. There're casseroles in the fridge. Whatever's easiest to reach will suit me." He rolled the scooter to the table and shifted onto a chair. He was getting better at that too.

Chet opened the refrigerator. "Did Ken tell you a bunch of the guys put together a schedule? We'll take turns coming over to feed the horses and anything else you need done until those casts come off. Somebody in the morning. Somebody in late afternoon or early evening."

"Yeah. Ken told me. He called earlier today with the information. I sure appreciate it. Wish I didn't have to ask."

"It isn't like you haven't helped others when they were in a bind." Chet put a plate with food on it into the microwave. He studied the keypad for a few moments, then punched in the time and pressed Start. While he waited for the food to get hot, he turned toward Buck again. "Seems to me, sometimes God wants us to learn the lesson of how to accept the generosity of others." He looked meaningfully at Buck. "It's a hard lesson for some of us."

Buck nodded.

Chet leaned his backside against the counter. "You've made some nice improvements to the outbuildings. I was out here once before you bought the place and saw the condition they were in."

"Haven't done all that much. But the horses will have better shelter come next winter."

"Maybe you did more than you think." The microwave dinged, and Chet turned to remove the plate of food. He was taking a knife and fork from the drawer when a knock sounded at the front door. "You eat. I'll see who it is." He set the plate on the table in front of Buck and walked to the living room. A few moments later, he returned alone.

"Who was it?"

"Charity Anderson. I hardly recognized her."

"Yeah, she's changed a lot since I saw her last. But that's been years."

"No, it was more than that. She seemed upset. Looked to me like she'd been crying."

Buck shifted on his chair. "Did she say what was wrong?"

"Nope. Just asked if you needed her to fix you dinner. I told her you were eating already. She said to tell you that she'll check in with you tomorrow morning."

Buck frowned. It had been a good eight hours since she'd left his place. She hadn't been any too pleased with him, but he hadn't done or said anything that would make her cry, especially not all this while later. Had he?

He gave his head a shake. He'd only spoken the truth. Her parents were hurt that she almost never came to see them. Buck didn't even know the Andersons all that well, and even he'd picked up on their feelings. They were good people. They deserved better from their youngest daughter.

"Your food's getting cold," Chet said, intruding on his thoughts.

"Yeah." He awkwardly speared some elbow macaroni with the fork in his left hand and brought it to his mouth. After swallowing, he said, "Thanks for warming it up. Now you'd better get home before your own dinner gets cold."

Chet chuckled. "You're right. I'd better." He turned to leave.

"Hey. I almost forgot. I finished that saddle you ordered. It's over at Antton's shop. You can get it anytime you want."

His friend's face brightened. "That's great news. Thanks."

Buck held up his right hand. "I won't be able to finish the bridle until this thing comes off."

"Don't worry about that. Kimberly will love the bridle whenever I give it to her." Chet waved and let himself out.

"Kimberly will love the bridle whenever I give it to her."

For some reason Chet's parting comment stayed with Buck as he ate his solitary meal in his solitary house.

Chapter 5

By THE NEXT DAY, Buck's ONE-HANDED SCOOTER skills had improved noticeably. Leaving the house unaided was still impossible and driving was out of the question until both casts came off. Cabin fever might become a problem before then, but it was manageable for now.

He was rolling his way into the living room when he heard the sound of a car door. He went to the window and saw his nieces and nephew as they hopped out of the back of their dad's minivan. His sister-in-law, Sara, was a little slower to disembark. Ken took her arm as they walked toward the front door, his other arm around her back. There was great tenderness in the gesture, and seeing it tugged at Buck's heart. It reminded him, more than a little, of his parents, back before the cancer.

Which also reminded him of the primary reason he preferred to stay single. It was dangerous to love. The heartache was too great when loss followed—and loss followed all too often. He couldn't help loving his family members. He couldn't help caring about his close friends. But he could protect himself from the kind of pain his mom had gone through after his dad died.

Ten-year-old Jake barged into the house without knocking. "Hey, Uncle Buck."

"Hey, Jake."

"How're you feeling?"

"Better today. Thanks."

His nieces, Krista and Sharon, entered next. Thirteen and twelve respectively, they were in an interesting phase— one that was foreign to their uncle. Not all that long ago they'd idolized Buck, but he'd somehow become antiquated in their eyes. He was thirty years old and over the hill. Wasn't that a bad joke from the seventies?

"Afternoon, girls," he said, trying to force interaction.

They mumbled some sort of response in unison before disappearing into the kitchen.

"Good to see you too." He grinned.

His brother and sister-in-law came through the open doorway at last, Sara moving awkwardly, more waddle than walk. She came straight to Buck and kissed his unshaven cheek. Then she rubbed her fingertips over the growth of facial hair. "This is new."

"Don't you like it?"

"Not especially."

He held up his right hand, showing her the cast. "Can't manage a razor. I'm afraid I'd cut my throat if I tried it left-handed."

"Mmm."

Ken said, "You're looking a lot better."

"Feel better too. And I'm getting the hang of this thing." He patted the handlebar on the scooter. "Great invention. I'd be in a lot of trouble without it."

Ken helped Sara ease herself down onto a chair. "The kids and I are going out to see to the chores. Anything special you want us to take care of?"

Buck shook his head.

"Jake. Girls. Come on. We need to feed and water the horses."

"*Dad*," Sharon and Krista said in identical whines. But they got up from the chairs at the kitchen table and followed their father and brother out the back door.

Buck sat on the sofa and propped his leg, mindful of the doctor's instructions to keep it elevated as much as possible. "I'm surprised you came over with Ken. I thought you were on bed rest."

"I am, most of the time. But I didn't think a little outing would be amiss as long as I'm careful. I'm more tired from doing nothing and going nowhere than anything else."

"I can relate to that." Buck didn't say it aloud, but strain was stamped across Sara's face. No wonder Ken was concerned. "How much longer have you got?"

"Six weeks, if I can hold out that long. The baby's on the small side, so every day I don't go into labor matters."

"Wish I could do something to help."

Sara offered a grateful smile. "With any luck, you'll be out of those casts before our little one arrives."

"You still don't know the sex?"

"Ken knows, but I won't let him or the doctor tell me or anyone else. I like to be surprised." She shrugged. "Sounds very old-fashioned, I suppose."

"No. I think I understand."

They fell into an easy silence, neither of them feeling compelled to talk just for the sake of talking. A benefit of having known each other for a quarter of a century or more. After a short while, Sara closed her eyes and seemed to relax into the quiet. She didn't get to enjoy it for long. The telephone rang, and Buck grabbed for it, although Sara's eyes were already open again.

"Hello."

"Hi, Buck. It's Charity."

"Good morning."

"Sorry I'm late checking in. I see that you've got company. Do you need me to come over and get your breakfast?"

He opened his mouth to say she didn't have to come, then thought better of it. "I'd appreciate it if you could. Ken's here feeding the horses so he's kind of busy. And Sara's a little off her game."

"Sara? Isn't she supposed to be on bed rest?"

"That's exactly what I asked her." He shot a pointed look in his sister-in-law's direction.

Sara stuck out her tongue in return.

"I'll be right over," Charity said. "Do you care if I bring Cocoa with me? I can leave her on your doorstep."

"Don't mind if she comes in. It's about time she and I met, don't you think? Just come on in when you get here. Door's open."

CHARITY PUSHED THE END BUTTON AND SET DOWN the phone. "Time for me to check on the patient next door, Cocoa. Want to come along this time?"

Anticipating an outing, the dog raced from the room.

"Well, I guess that answers that." Charity smiled—grateful for a pet that could make her do so.

A short while later, she and Cocoa stood on Buck's stoop. She rapped softly before opening the door. Buck was on the sofa, leg elevated. Sara Malone was in a nearby chair.

"Sit, Cocoa," Charity commanded. Then she walked over to the chair. As she bent down to kiss Sara's cheek, she asked, "How're you doing?"

"Not bad." Sara smiled briefly.

It didn't look to Charity as if she was telling the truth. There were dark smudges under the other woman's eyes and her face looked drawn.

"It's good to see you, Charity. It's always so long between times."

"I know."

"I'm glad you're here for the summer. You know we've got a big all-class reunion coming up."

"Yeah. I got the letter about it."

"Well, you won't have an excuse to miss this one."

Does Jon still come to the reunions? The thought sent a shudder running down her spine. She didn't want to think about him. Her outing yesterday had stirred up too many unwelcome feelings. Another day of the same would be unbearable.

Charity looked toward Buck, whose eyes had narrowed thoughtfully as he watched the conversation. "Anything special you want to eat?"

"Whatever's easy," he answered.

But there was something in his gaze that made her think he could see her secrets. The feeling of transparency made her anxious. With a jerky nod, she swung around and went into the kitchen.

From the living room, she heard Buck say, "Come, Cocoa. Come here, girl. Let's you and me officially meet." Knowing she would have to give the command to release Cocoa before the dog would move, she turned.

Only she was wrong. Cocoa was already headed toward the sofa, toenails clicking on the wood floor.

When Cocoa reached him, Buck cupped the dog's muzzle with his good hand and looked her straight in the eyes. "So you're the one who caused all of this."

Cocoa wagged her tail, as if accepting a compliment.

"Maybe you could try not to do that again. It's embarrassing to be knocked over in front of a pretty woman."

What? It shouldn't matter that Buck Malone thought her pretty. It *didn't* matter that he thought so. And yet, for only a moment, a tingle of pleasure replaced her anxiety.

Buck raised his voice while still looking at the dog. "She's got a strong, powerful head. Smart as a whip, isn't she?"

Drawn a couple of steps toward the living room, Charity nodded. "She is."

"I'll bet she's got some American Staffordshire terrier in her."

"Along with several other breeds."

Buck leaned against the back of the sofa. "My last dog was a border collie. His name was Snap. Had him since the summer after I graduated from high school. He died this spring.

Too late in the season for me to get a puppy. Wouldn't be old enough to go on the trail with me, and training takes time." He glanced at his right leg. "Not that that matters now. I won't be guiding anybody into the backcountry anytime too soon."

Perhaps sensing she was responsible for the change in Buck's tone of voice, Cocoa placed her muzzle next to his thigh and looked up at him. Buck laughed softly, a pleasant sound.

Was he as nice as others thought him? Charity wondered. Or was he more like some of his friends? Or one friend in particular?

Don't. Don't. Don't.

The back screen door slammed shut, and a young boy of about nine or ten darted into the kitchen. When he saw Charity, he screeched to a halt.

"Who're you?" he demanded

Sara had laid her head back in her chair, resting, but at that, she cracked open an eye. "Jake!" Her tone brooked no argument. "Mind your manners."

"Sorry."

But Charity wasn't really listening. As soon as Jake had hit the door, she'd frozen, her heart seizing before stuttering into a painful rhythm as she stared at the boy before her. He was young. About . . .

Ten. He looks like he's ten. The same as—

No. She would *not* do this. Ignoring Jake's quizzical look, she turned away. Her hands shook and she wiped them on her thighs. She would finish what she'd come for and leave. She would keep her emotions hidden.

Buck had said he would eat whatever was easy. That's exactly what she would give him. Two scrambled eggs, a piece of buttered toast, and a glass of orange juice. She could prepare that in a matter of minutes.

The back screen door creaked open a second time. When Charity looked to her right, she saw two girls—Sara and Ken's daughters, obviously. Girls in the process of becoming young women. They mumbled a hello before moving on to the living room. Then their father stepped into view.

"Morning, Charity." Ken glanced at the stovetop. "I should have let you know I could fix breakfast for Buck this morning. Sorry I didn't think to send one of the kids over to tell you."

Children's laughter drifted in from the other room, and Charity felt another painful stab in her chest. "It's all right," she said, her voice breaking. She cleared her throat. "You were busy. Just let me finish cooking, and I'll be out of here."

"You don't have to rush."

"Actually, I do. I have work waiting for me at home."

Work . . . and a need to escape the warm family scene going on in the other room.

When the door closed behind Charity and her dog a short while later, Buck looked at Sara. "Did she seem upset to you?"

"It's hard to say." Sara gave a small shrug. "A lot of years have passed since I hung out with Charity, and that was only because she was Terri's little sister. She kept to herself most of the time. In college and after, I heard she became quite a party girl. That was difficult for me to believe, but I guess it was true." A frown furrowed her brow. "Now she's a successful author. She seems to have pulled her life together. At least in the obvious ways. But she really turned her back on Kings Meadow and all the people who knew her when. Terri worries about her. I know that for certain. So do her folks, although they've never said so to me."

It was more information than Buck had expected to get from Sara, and he found himself intrigued by it. The day of the accident, while he was with Charity in the parking lot, he'd thought she disliked him or at least wanted him to leave her alone. But maybe it was something bigger than that. Something not about him in particular but about Kings Meadow in general.

Ken stepped into view. "Charity put your breakfast on the table. Want me to bring it to you?"

"No thanks, bro. I'll eat in the kitchen." Buck pushed on the arm of the sofa with his left hand until he was upright enough to move his knee to the scooter. "Man, this is a pain," he muttered to himself.

Sara heard him and laughed softly. "I'd trade you if I could." She rubbed her belly in a circular motion. "Six weeks of those casts or, hopefully, six weeks of this."

"No, thanks. Don't think I'd care for that trade." He grinned at her as he rolled toward the kitchen.

"You can bet you wouldn't," Sara retorted.

As Buck got settled at the table, Ken said, "I think I'd better get Sara home. Do you need anything else before we go?"

"Nah. I'm good. Thanks for the help."

Ken punched him in the upper arm, a gesture that said more about the love between brothers than any words could.

Chapter 6

In Boise on a Friday night, Charity had rarely stayed at home. She usually went out to dinner with a date or to see a movie with girlfriends or dancing with a group of singles. When with others, she could escape the memories she wanted to avoid, memories she'd run from for years.

She had fewer choices in Kings Meadow. She could go to one of the bars, but those places were smoky and noisy. And besides, she'd stopped drinking once she admitted the part alcohol had played in her numerous bad choices. She could go out to eat at the Tamarack Grill. They had good food, but there would also be too many people who knew her. Too many people with too many comments and questions.

No, it was better that she stay put. Except her parents' home felt so quiet and empty, and the silence wasn't comfortable. It gave her too much time to think. To think about the past. An even bigger problem here in Kings Meadow than when she was in Boise. She'd had enough grim thoughts for one day.

I could cook a real dinner for Buck.

Where had that thought come from? No, that wouldn't be wise.

Why not? If I don't cook, I'll go over there and heat another helping of a casserole. Does he deserve more of the same, day after day?

Besides, Buck wasn't at fault for the memories that troubled her any more than his nephew was at fault for her reaction to him that morning. Guilt by association. That wasn't fair.

And besides, I like to cook.

She released a deep sigh.

She had spent the better part of the last year trying to change the things that were wrong with her and wrong with the ways she had lived. She'd grown tired of . . . of everything. Mostly she was tired of the fear that had let her past rule her present.

Her mind made up, she went into the kitchen and removed items from the refrigerator: salmon—although she had shopped for one, she'd bought enough for two—a couple of potatoes, and the makings for a tossed salad. She reached to turn on the oven, then pulled back her hand. If she did the cooking here, she would still be surrounded by the silence that troubled her. No, she would prepare the dinner at Buck's house. Maybe he would be even more impressed by her culinary skills.

She and Nathan Gilbert, her last boyfriend, had frequently enjoyed candlelight dinners in her home. She'd thought for a short while that they might marry, but Nathan hadn't been impressed by her efforts to put her life in order. He wasn't interested in settling down. Not with her. Not with anyone. She couldn't even lay the blame entirely at his feet. For years she'd broken off every relationship the moment it looked like the man in her life was getting too serious. She'd never let herself fall in love. Perhaps she hadn't been able to love. But now . . . perhaps she'd like to have a chance of loving and being loved.

Shaking off those thoughts, she put the dinner preparations into a basket and headed out the door, Cocoa following close behind. Buck's driveway was empty of any vehicles save his truck. Had a friend already been there to feed the horses or was someone still to come?

She knocked as usual. When she heard him call, "Come in," she turned the knob and opened the door.

"Is Cocoa welcome?" she asked before stepping inside.

"Of course. She and I made peace this morning." Buck was seated on the sofa where he'd been that morning as she departed. He pointed at the basket. "What've you got there?"

"Dinner."

He cocked an eyebrow in question.

"I figured you must be tired already of warmed-up casseroles. How does baked salmon sound?"

"Delicious. But that's a lot of trouble for you to go to."

"Not really. I have to eat, too, you know."

He grinned. "You're going to eat with me?"

She felt his smile in the pit of her stomach, the sensation completely unexpected and entirely unwelcome. "Yes." She turned toward the kitchen. *Careful. He's just a neighbor in need.*

Charity set the basket on the table and withdrew the two potatoes. It wasn't long before they were baking in the oven. With that done, she tried to find the right pans and bowls and knives for the remainder of the meal preparation. Charity's kitchen in Boise had a specific place for everything. So did her mother's. Buck's cupboards were—to put it kindly—less organized, and it took quite awhile to find some of the items she wanted, even after having used his kitchen several times.

Finally, everything she needed was on the countertops, and she went to work on the salad, chopping and slicing and mixing. When it was ready, she placed the salad bowl in the refrigerator next to the paper-wrapped salmon. In short order, she'd cleaned up after herself with a damp dishcloth.

"Anything I can do to help?" Buck asked, his voice much closer than the living room.

Surprised, Charity spun to face him.

Buck didn't seem to notice he'd startled her as he rolled his scooter toward the cupboard that held plates, bowls, and glasses. "I can at least set the table. It's good for me to get off the couch."

Had the kitchen shrunk in size in the last few moments? It seemed so with him in it.

Stretching up, Buck took two dinner plates from the cupboard and set them in the basket on the front of the scooter. A couple of drinking glasses followed. Two sets of silverware went into one of the glasses.

"You're getting quite accomplished at that," Charity said.

"Maybe boredom is the real mother of invention." He shot a grin over his shoulder. "You know. Instead of necessity."

Once again, his smile brought a shiver of pleasure. *Not good. Really not good.* She was trying to turn her life around and had been making progress. She wanted stability, a future, and if God was willing, a family. But she didn't want to find it here in Kings Meadow, and she wouldn't find it with a man like Buck Malone.

Without a word, she turned away and got back to cooking.

Buck wasn't used to working this hard to win a woman's interest. It frustrated him. It also made him all the more determined to break down those defenses of hers or know the reason why.

He rolled toward the table. "Tell me about your writing." That seemed a safe topic. "What got you started?"

There was a lengthy silence, and he wondered if she would refuse to answer. Had he made her that angry this morning? He glanced toward the stove and found her back to him.

But finally, she turned. "The short version: I wrote my first book on a dare from Terri." She shrugged. "I never knew I wanted to write a book until I did it. And afterward I couldn't imagine wanting to do anything else."

A dozen or so years ago, Buck had had dreams for his future. He'd planned to go to college, and then he'd hoped to play professional baseball. He'd wanted to travel, to see the world. Lots of choices had seemed to stretch before him. Time and circumstances had obliterated most of them.

But he wasn't bitter about the way things had turned out. He'd done what had to be done. He'd taken care of the people he loved. Now he had a simple, uncomplicated, uncluttered life. He liked it that way. He didn't lack anything that he needed, and his wants were few.

"What about you?" Charity asked.

He had to stop for a moment to figure out what she was asking. Then he mirrored her earlier shrug. "I sort of fell into guiding. Needed work and got hired on by an outfitter out of Cascade. Eventually I decided to work for myself."

"And you never aspired to do anything else?"

"Not really." The last thing he wanted was for Charity

to pity him. If she didn't know what had happened to his dad and the events that had followed, then he'd just as soon keep it that way. "I mean, nothing that matters much in the overall scheme of things. I've got a good life. I don't see any reason to change it." He removed the plates and glasses from the basket on the scooter and slid them to opposite sides of the table.

"Did you ever . . . Did you ever want to get married?" she asked.

"No." The word sounded sharp in his ears. He looked toward her again and tried to soften the next one. "You?"

An expression he couldn't define flittered across her face. Wistful? Painful? Fearful? Something. "I didn't want marriage for a long time. I wanted to be on my own. It was better that way. But lately I've had a change of heart. If I . . . If I could find the right man, yes, I'd like to get married."

"Have you got somebody in mind?" In Buck's experience, most women had somebody in mind when they asked about marriage. Several local gals had thought he was the one for them. It had taken some convincing to change their minds. All of them were now married to other guys and he was happy for them—and happy for himself.

"No," Charity answered after a few moments of silence. "Nobody in mind. I was in a relationship with a man named Nathan for over a year." She shrugged a second time. "It didn't work out, and we stopped seeing each other this past spring. I haven't done any dating since then. I've been sort of . . . reevaluating."

He wondered if Nathan was the cause of the sadness he sometimes saw in her eyes. He hoped not. She didn't look sad right now. Still, he had a sudden distaste for the fellow, whoever he was. He had to be an idiot to have let Charity get away.

Uneasiness washed over Buck, although he couldn't pinpoint the cause. It was followed by another wave of frustration over his current circumstances. He was trapped inside the house, unable to get out, unable to work, unable to even spend time with the horses. The days and weeks of his confinement—or at the very least his dependence upon others—stretched before him like an unending parade.

CHARITY TURNED TO THE REFRIGERATOR AND WITH-drew the salmon. After seasoning the fish with coarse-grained salt and ground black paper, she placed it skin side down in a nonstick pan. The pan went straight into the oven on the rack above the potatoes. By the time she turned around, Buck was no longer in the kitchen—and it bothered her that he was gone. It bothered her even more that it bothered her.

She walked to the living room entrance. Buck was back on the sofa, left hand on Cocoa's head while the fingers of his right hand tried to scratch a spot beneath the cast on his leg. "Dinner will be ready in about fifteen minutes."

He looked at her. "It already smells good."

Not knowing what else to do with herself until the fish and potatoes were ready to come out of the oven, she went to the nearest chair and sat on it. Not for the first time, her gaze roamed the living room. There weren't any feminine touches anywhere. It was a man's domain, without knickknacks or unnecessary adornment. A fine layer of dust lay on all flat surfaces; she was tempted to do something about that.

Then she remembered the framed photographs on a shelf in a bookcase that was mostly empty of books. She'd noticed them a couple of days ago but hadn't taken the time to look at them. Curious now, she got up and crossed to the bookcase.

On the far left were a couple of family photos from when Ken and Buck were still young kids, both of them taken in the outdoors, one of them with Buck showing off a large trout. Buck's senior photo was next to that one. He looked the way she remembered him best—handsome, self-confident, and full of youthful exuberance. Next to it was one of Buck on horseback, brown cowboy hat shading his face. A string of packhorses followed behind him, and tall pines framed both sides of the trail. The final photograph was an eight-by-ten of his parents on their wedding day. Where were they now? she wondered. Had someone told her and she'd forgotten? Obviously they weren't in Kings Meadow or they would have been the ones looking after their son.

The telephone rang, shattering the silence that had filled the living room.

Buck grabbed the handset. "Hello . . . Oh no. Sorry to hear that . . . I understand. Can't be helped . . . Don't worry about it. I'll find somebody . . . No, don't bother. Really. It's all good . . . Okay. Talk to you later." He ended the call and glanced toward Charity. "My friend's got a sick kid and can't come feed the horses tonight. I'll have to call around to find somebody else to do it."

The way he said it revealed his intense dislike for asking for help. She empathized. "I can do it," she said as she stepped away from the bookcase.

"Oh, no. That's asking too much."

"You didn't ask, Buck. I offered."

"Are you sure?"

"I'm sure. I like horses. Always have. You'll just have to tell me what's on the menu for them." She stood. "But we get to eat first because our dinner is about to come out of the oven."

"You won't have to tell me twice," he said, reaching for the handlebar of the scooter.

Charity went into the kitchen, arriving at the stove as the timer buzzed. In no time at all she had their meal on the table. Buck asked if it was all right for him to bless the food. That surprised her. She didn't remember him being much of a churchgoer back in high school. Then again, she hadn't been much of one once she started college. Only recently had she begun to look for a church to attend.

He's changed. So have I. At least a little.

After the prayer, Buck stabbed the salmon with the fork in his left hand. Fortunately, no knife was required. He brought the fish to his mouth, closed his eyes as he chewed and swallowed, then released a satisfied, "Mmmmm."

The pleasure she felt in that moment was all out of proportion for what the sound deserved, but it stayed with her for the remainder of the evening. Through dinner. Through feeding the horses. Through washing the dishes. Through going home, checking and answering her e-mail, watching a movie, washing her face and brushing her teeth, and getting into bed. And that night, for the first time since her arrival in Kings Meadow, her sleep was undisturbed by bad dreams.

Chapter 7

OVER THE NEXT WEEK, CHARITY SPENT LONG HOURS at her computer, writing hard on the new novel. Buck didn't require a lot of her time. His brother and friends had taken over the job of fixing him breakfast and warming up something for his dinner, so she had no excuse to break away from her work. Sometimes she wished she did, for she still didn't feel that special connection with her story.

Finally, she decided to call her editor in New York.

"Bridget Steele."

"Good morning, Bridget. It's Charity Anderson."

"Hello, Charity. How are you?"

"Fine, thanks."

"Are you still staying at your parents' home in the mountains like you thought you would?"

"Yes. I'll be here all summer."

"Remodeling coming along okay on your house?"

Charity nodded as she answered, "Yes."

"That's good. So tell me: how's the book coming?"

Charity had known that would be the next question. The voice in her head screamed for her to lie, but she didn't. "Not as well as I'd like. That's why I called. Maybe I can't write a romance."

There was silence on the other end of the line. Long enough to make Charity's pulse hum with dread.

But finally, Bridget said, "Tell me about the place where you grew up."

"Kings Meadow?"

"Yes, describe it to me. Make me see it in my mind."

Charity rose from her chair and went to the window. From there, she saw several horses grazing in the pasture behind Buck's house. "It's a small town surrounded on all sides by mountains. The high valley where it's set is shaped like a boomerang. It had fewer than three thousand residents when I graduated from high school. I doubt it's grown any since then. There are pine trees all over the mountains. Lodge pole and ponderosa. The valley floor is the deep green of emeralds in June and spotted with colorful wildflowers. Most everybody here owns horses. Lots of cowboys and cowgirls wherever you look. Country music on most of the radios."

"Cowboys. They're always popular in romance novels. They make good heroes, and I believe that the author finding the right hero is key to making everything else fall into place."

Charity gave her head a slow shake. She hadn't hung out with anyone she would call a cowboy in over a decade. Not that she wouldn't still love to ride horses or even attend a rodeo. She would. But her lifestyle didn't allow for those things.

"Why not write about someone you know? Or at least someone you could use as inspiration for the hero of your story."

Immediately she pictured Buck. Not on a scooter with casts on ankle and wrist, but as she'd seen him in the parking lot of the Merc before he fell. Despite all the reasons it shouldn't, her heart fluttered at the image in her head. Boots, jeans, and cowboy hat. Tall and lean. A slow, lazy kind of smile. Brown eyes that conveyed an easy-going nature. Even more good-looking than he'd been in high school, she'd finally decided. Hero material for the taking.

"Charity?"

"Yes, I'm here."

"Do you know someone like that?"

"Actually, yes. I do. He lives next door to my parents." Charity wouldn't mention that she'd had a serious teenage crush on him.

"Is he a cowboy?"

"A wilderness guide for four or five months of the year. A saddle maker in the winter."

"And is he nice? Is he likable?"

"Yes."

"Handsome?"

Another flutter in Charity's chest. "Uh . . . yes. Most women would think so."

"Do *you* think so?" her editor pressed.

She drew in a quick breath before answering, "Yes."

"Well then. Sounds like you have the inspiration for your hero. Now all you need is the right heroine and a difficult situation that threatens to keep them apart."

Bridget made it sound so easy. But it wasn't easy. Wouldn't be easy. Even with Buck as the blueprint for her hero.

"Let's keep brainstorming, Charity. I know you can do this. You're a talented writer. We just need to get you over the hump. Can you use what you've already written with a new hero? Maybe a new setting? One that looks like Kings Meadow."

"I think so." Charity returned to the desk, flipped open her notebook, and prepared to jot down whatever ideas she and Bridget came up with.

* * *

More than an hour later, Charity pressed the End button and set the phone on the desk. Her head throbbed as her thoughts tumbled into a mixed-up mess. Cocoa whimpered at her from the doorway, and that was all Charity needed for an excuse to leave her desk and get outside for some fresh air. Hopefully she'd get enough fresh air to make the headache go away.

"Let's go, girl."

The morning was pleasant. Not too warm yet, although the temperature was climbing. The sky was an unbroken expanse of blue. Not a single cloud to be seen. Mistress and dog set off at a brisk pace down the road, heading east, away from town. Houses were few and far between. After the last one, there was nothing for another two miles on either side of the road but fenced pastures. Then the road came to an end. Horses dotted the land wherever she looked. Mixed in was the occasional cow or goat and even a couple of llamas.

By the time they reached the dead end, the walk had worked

its magic. Charity's headache was gone. Not only that but her confusion and frustration had been driven out as well. She wasn't fooled. When she opened her laptop again, the action might bring headache, confusion, and/or frustration rushing back. But for now, she enjoyed the sense of calm that filled her.

She remembered Terri telling her that she needed to relax and forget about the book for a while. She hadn't followed her sister's advice. She'd tried to write something—*anything*—every day since she arrived in Kings Meadow. How much worse could it be if she simply took a week off and let the story simmer?

"But what would make me relax and forget the book?" she whispered.

Immediately she thought of Buck's horses. They were being fed daily, but no one was riding them. They must need exercise. Maybe getting into the saddle would put her in the mood to write a cowboy romance.

"It couldn't hurt to try." Could it?

Especially since Buck Malone was supposed to inspire her love story. In a fictional sense, of course. Not for real.

BUCK STARED AT THE CAST ON HIS WRIST AND WISHED he could bust out of it. But he knew better. The bones were just beginning to knit. He needed to follow doctor's orders for a few more weeks. It would be difficult to make saddles with a bum right hand, and he wouldn't be of much use as a guide either. Not when it came to setting up and breaking down camps. Not when it came to swinging an ax or having strength in an emergency situation.

Patience. He had to exercise patience.

He rolled the scooter to the large window in the living room and looked south toward the river and the mountains beyond it. What he wouldn't give to be outside on this fine day. The boredom grew worse by the minute. He eyed the steps leading down from his front door. If he was careful, maybe he could maneuver down them on the scooter.

With a *woof*, Cocoa came racing across his front yard. The dog stopped on the front stoop and looked at Buck through the glass, silently asking for admittance. Buck chuckled. Cocoa seemed to like him a lot. He was even beginning to believe Charity had warmed to him a little. Speaking of whom, there she came, following the dog at a slower pace. Instead of the shorts and slip-on sneakers he'd seen her in several times, she wore jeans and boots. It was a good look on her. But then, she would look good in just about anything.

Buck rolled to the front door and opened it. "Hey, Cocoa." He patted the dog's head, then lifted his gaze. "Hey, Charity. Nice morning."

"Yes." She stopped on the stone walkway. "It's beautiful out."

"Think you could help me get outside? I've got cabin fever something fierce."

The request seemed to trouble her. "I suppose we could try. If you're sure you should. I'd hate to be the cause of another fall."

He gave her a hard look. She was a slight thing, true. But she was stronger than she looked.

"Maybe you should wait until your brother or one of your friends comes over to see to the horses."

"Nobody'll come again until this evening. I need outside now."

Charity worried her lower lips with her teeth.

"Help me out the back door to the patio." Buck sensed her weakening. "Half an hour in the sunshine will do me a world of good."

There was a long silence before she said, "Okay. I hope you don't regret it."

Buck backed out of the doorway, a silent invitation for her to enter. After a brief hesitation, she did so. Giving her no chance to change her mind, Buck turned the scooter and headed for the kitchen exit. He heard the click of Cocoa's claws on the floor, then the sounds of Charity's boots. He stopped the scooter and reached for the doorknob before rolling through the open doorway.

"Here," Charity said as she stopped at his side on the back stoop.

He looked at her, and she held out a crutch to him. "I thought we'd use the scooter," he said.

"No." She shook her head. "The crutch is better. Better without wheels as you go down, I think. I'll steady you from the other side." She glanced at the patio. "Let me bring one of those chairs closer first." With a little push, she forced him to take hold of the crutch before she went down the steps. She dragged a hard plastic chair across the patio and left it near the bottom of the steps, then returned to his side. "Ready?"

"More than ready." He draped his right arm over her shoulders while she put her left arm around his lower back.

It turned out to be easier than either of them expected. Much easier than the day his brother had brought him home from the clinic, but he'd been doped up at the time. Today he was completely clear headed.

Between the crutch and Charity's steady presence, Buck reached his destination without any threat of a fall. Still, he was glad to sit in the chair. Charity took the crutch and laid it behind him. Cocoa came around and sat at his left side—which he suspected annoyed Charity a little, the way her dog had taken to him. He did his best to conceal his amusement.

"Buck? Could I ask a favor?"

He squinted up at her, the sun bright in his eyes. She moved a little to her right to shade him.

"Thanks," he said. "What's the favor?"

"I was wondering if I might ride one of your horses. I haven't had an opportunity to ride in ages."

So that was the reason for the jeans and boots. "Mind?" He cocked an eyebrow. "You'd be doing me another big favor. You can ride anytime you want. Every day if you want. Any horse you choose. The more, the better. They'll get fat and lazy if they stand around much longer."

She smiled, and it was as if the sunshine she was trying to block came right through her to blind him with its brilliance. His breath caught in his chest, and he looked away from her. "Anything you might need's in the tack shed there. Key's inside the back door, hanging on a nail."

"Thanks. I appreciate it. I'm hoping if I spend some time in the saddle it will get my creativity flowing again."

"Having trouble with the book?"

"Sort of." She sighed. "It's so different from the books I wrote before. Changing my style has shaken my confidence.

But I talked to my editor this morning, and she had a few suggestions."

"Good ones, I trust."

She looked at him for a long while before answering. There was something about her gaze, the slight tip of her head to one side, that made him feel . . . peculiar. Then she offered him another smile. "Yes. I think they are good ideas." The odd feeling went away.

"I admire what you do. I never was much good with words. Never been the creative type."

"That's not true, Buck. I saw one of your saddles awhile back. It was beautiful."

"Making saddles keeps the winters from feeling too long." He shrugged away the compliment, pretending it didn't please him, though it did. "What you do is different. Takes brains to be a writer."

"You were a good student back in high school. Didn't you get a scholarship to college?"

"For sports. Not for academics. I about killed myself for every A that I got in high school." He shrugged. "Didn't make any difference since I never went on to college."

"Why didn't you go? I thought you would."

"Just didn't work out." He motioned with his head toward the pasture. "You'd better have that ride."

After a brief silence, Charity said, "Okay. I won't be long."

"Take as long as you want. I'll be fine. It's not too hot. Feels good to be outside."

With a nod, she stepped around him. After retrieving the key from inside the back door, she walked toward the tack shed. Cocoa sat up, glanced from her mistress to Buck, then lay down again.

CHARITY'S HORSEBACK RIDE THAT MORNING DID more for improving her outlook than she'd expected. She didn't even mind that Cocoa chose to stay with Buck. Well, maybe she minded a little.

The traitor.

Grinning at the thought, she rode the black gelding back toward the pasture gate. When she glanced in the direction of the patio, Buck raised his left hand in silent acknowledgment that he'd seen and been seen. Both he and the dog were exactly where they'd been when she rode away more than an hour before. She'd intended to ride about thirty minutes, tops, but once in the saddle she'd had a hard time turning the horse around.

With swift efficiency, she unsaddled the gelding, brushed him, and turned him out with the other horses. She was still smiling as she strode toward the patio.

Buck shaded his eyes. "Looks good on you."

"What does?" She stopped before his chair.

"Not sure. Like there's a new lift in your walk. Less weight on your shoulders."

Charity wasn't sure she liked Buck's ability to read her so easily.

He grinned. "Maybe it's those fancy new boots of yours that make the difference."

She glanced down at her feet. They *were* new boots— bought for fashion rather than riding—but they didn't look new at the moment, covered in dust, tiny flecks of hay and grass, and perhaps a little horse manure.

Before she could answer, he spoke again. "Maybe it's time for me to go back inside. I think I got enough sun for today. Should've grabbed my hat on the way out."

"Of course." Come to think of it, his forehead and nose did look a bit red. "I'm sorry. I shouldn't have ridden for so long."

"Nah. Don't feel bad. I'm glad you enjoyed yourself." His smile said he meant it.

The heroes in romance novels must do that too. Say the right words and then punctuate them with a smile. And maybe the heroines felt that same little shiver of pleasure that had run up her spine.

Uh-oh.

She reached for the crutch and in no time at all had Buck safely up the few steps and into the house.

Chapter 8

CHARITY PRESSED HER FOREHEAD AGAINST THE
gelding's neck and breathed in the horsey smell. It was like
therapy, only better, being around horses again, riding again.
Why hadn't she realized how much she'd missed this? As a
kid, she'd spent as many hours as possible on the back of a
horse. Competing hadn't interested her. No 4-H shows or
barrel racing for her. She'd been happy just to ride all over
this valley and on trails in the mountains.

She'd been riding Buck's horses every day since that first
afternoon, taking turns with the animals and feeling out
their personalities. Today she'd returned to her favorite, the
black one she'd first ridden.

Knowing she'd spent enough time with him already, she
gave the horse one final pat and then left the pasture. When
she glanced toward the patio, she was surprised to see Buck
and Cocoa weren't alone now. A few strides closer and she
realized who the woman was: Ashley Holloway. She'd been

Buck's steady girlfriend for much of their senior year way back when. Popular and beautiful—and, in Charity's opinion, rather empty-headed—she'd left the U of I after a couple of years to marry a successful investment broker from McCall.

Charity hadn't seen Ashley since the summer after their high school graduation. As she drew closer to the patio, it became clear that the other woman had only grown more beautiful with time. And if the designer outfit she wore was any indication, reports of her husband's success weren't exaggerated.

Ashley looked away from Buck, saw Charity, and gave an excited squeal as she shot to her feet. "Charity Anderson! Is that you? Mom told me you're in town for the summer. I'm so glad to see you." She embraced Charity as if they were long lost friends. Impossible since they'd never been close in the first place.

It was such a surprise that Charity couldn't speak for a few moments, not even after she was free again.

"I came to town today," Ashley said, "because I'm working on the all-class reunion, and Mom told me about Buck's accident. I had to come over and wish him well." She turned toward him, leaned down, and patted his cheek. "Poor guy. My grandpa says if it weren't for bad luck you'd have no luck at all."

Buck shook his head. "It was an old *Hee Haw* song that said that, Ashley. Not your grandpa."

"Whatever." Ashley waved away his words with a flick of her hand. Then she looked at Charity again. "Are you coming to the reunion in August?"

First Sara and now Ashley. Were they ganging up on her? It felt like it. "I'm not sure."

"Oh, you simply must come. You must. You're in town anyway. I promise it's going to be loads of fun. And I would absolutely love to sit down and talk and catch up with you. I mean, who would've believed you would wind up being Kings Meadow's most famous graduate."

The sense of well-being Charity had felt after her horseback ride was beginning to evaporate. "I'll think about it, Ashley."

"You must come. You missed our tenth reunion."

Charity nodded but said nothing more. She wanted to leave, but she would have to help Buck inside first and was reluctant to do that while Ashley was still there.

"Well, I really can't stay," Ashley said, as if reading Charity's mind. "Lots to do and little time to do it in. You know how it is." She laughed airily before giving Buck a kiss on the cheek. "Later." Then she kissed Charity's cheek, too, and hurried off.

Charity turned toward Buck, stunned into silence a second time.

He looked as if he was holding back a laugh. "She's got a good heart, you know."

"Maybe. But I don't think she knew who I was in high school, and that was the last summer I saw her. What makes us such good buddies now?"

"Time."

That stopped her in her tracks. He was right, of course. Time changed all of them, for good or for bad. Hadn't she been trying to change herself for the better? So would it hurt to give Ashley the benefit of the doubt? She supposed not.

Buck had patiently waited out her internal struggle.

"Well," he said now, "maybe you'd best get me inside. I imagine you've got work waiting for you."

"Mmm."

"Wish I could say the same." He grabbed the crutch from the ground. "At least I've managed to cover all of the trips I had scheduled through the end of July. That's a load off my mind."

Before Charity could move to his right side to help him up, the telephone he'd placed in his shirt pocket rang.

"Hold on a sec," he said to her before answering it. "Hello?"

Charity watched his eyes widen as he listened.

"I'll be there. Soon as I can catch a ride . . . No, Ken. I'll be there."

"What is it?" Charity asked as soon as he hung up.

"Sara. She's gone into labor. They're taking her to Boise by ambulance."

"Ambulance," she repeated softly.

"Can you get me to the hospital? I need to be there for Ken."

Buck continued speaking, but Charity's brain had already shut down. The hospital. A baby on the way. A baby on the way too soon . . . Her body felt hot, then cold, as she fought to push back the memories that instantly flooded her mind. She had to keep control. *I will keep control. I will not lose it.*

Bit by bit, she fought her way back to the moment only to realize Buck had gone silent. He looked at her carefully. "Are you okay?"

She didn't trust her voice, so she nodded before answering.

"Give me five minutes to change my clothes. I'll drive my car over here to get you." She took a step toward her parents' house, then looked back. "Do you need to go inside before we leave?"

For a moment he looked as though he might press the issue, but he shook his head. "No, I'm good. You'll need to grab my scooter for me. That's all."

"Okay. I won't be long. Come on, Cocoa."

She jogged toward the house. She didn't allow herself to think beyond the need to hurry. She simply washed her hands and face and brushed her hair into a ponytail—noticing with detached calm the paleness of her face in the mirror, the ever-so-slight trembling of her hands—then changed into cropped pants and a cotton top. At the last minute she grabbed a sweater, in case the waiting area was cold. She remembered the cold . . .

On her way back through the kitchen, she scooped dry kibble into Cocoa's food bowl and made sure the dog had plenty of water.

"You be good, girl. I don't know how long I'll be." If it turned out to be too long, she would have to call someone to come over and let the dog out. But she couldn't worry about that now. She had to get Buck.

She drove her SUV around to the back of his house. Before helping him to the car, she went inside for his scooter. It was only a few more minutes before they were on their way. Neither spoke as they passed through town. Once beyond Kings Meadow, Charity was glad to have the winding river road to concentrate on. It kept her thoughts from wandering to the hospital and a baby coming before its time.

BUCK STARED OUT THE WINDOW, TOO BUSY PRAYING to notice the passing landscape. He asked God to protect Sara. He asked God to keep the baby safe. He asked for wisdom for the doctors and nurses, in the delivery room and in the nursery afterward. The baby was early. A preemie. But these days, a baby that came early had a good chance. Right?

Ken had told him he didn't have to come, but Buck wasn't about to stay home. Maybe he couldn't do anything but be there. So he would be there. He knew how to "be there."

I'm sick of "being there," God. Sick of dealing with bad situations. Please let this be a good one. Please let Sara and the baby be all right.

"Are you okay, Buck?"

He looked over at Charity. "Yeah. I'm fine. Just hoping Sara can say the same." He turned his gaze to the road ahead. "About another half an hour?"

"A little longer. Probably forty-five minutes to the hospital."

"Do you suppose the ambulance is there yet?"

"I'm sure of it. And I'm sure Sara and the baby are fine too."

He tried to appreciate the certainty in her voice and words. He tried to believe her. He almost did. Almost. But he needed to see for himself.

Just go faster. Faster. Faster. Faster. He pressed down on the floorboard with his left foot.

As if she'd read his mind, Charity said, "I'll be able to speed up once we're past the river."

He nodded, but his impatience didn't diminish. If he didn't have these stupid casts on, he would be at the wheel. He knew how to drive this road fast. He'd done it before.

It seemed an eternity before they reached the city limits, but finally they were on State Street and on a straight shot toward the hospital. Charity drove to the front entrance to let him and his scooter out.

"I'll park the car and then I'll find you," she called after him as he rolled toward the automatic doors.

At the information counter, he told the young woman that his sister-in-law was in labor and had been brought in by ambulance. The hospital employee—or perhaps she was a volunteer—looked down for a few moments, locating the information on the computer screen, then told him where he needed to go, pointing to the bank of elevators. She was still speaking as he sped toward them.

Buck hadn't been present for the births of his nieces. Ken had been in college at the time, and both of the girls had been born in Moscow near the university. Buck had missed his nephew's birth, too, although he'd been at the same hospital at the same time. Only he'd been over in oncology with his dad, watching a little more of his life draining out of him.

He ran into his brother in the hallway outside of the maternity wing. He'd barely stopped the scooter before Ken embraced him.

"I didn't think you'd get here this fast," his brother said in a gruff voice.

"Charity was with me when you called. She drove me."

Ken stepped back. "Thanks. I . . . I'm glad you came."

"How's Sara?"

"Doing all right for now. I had to step out of the delivery room to try to get my emotions under control. I don't want to upset her."

"What does the doctor say?"

"He expects the delivery to go well. He says the hospital has the state's most experienced Level III NICU. The baby will have the best care available. They've got rooms in the hospital for the parents to stay in as long as the baby has to be here."

Buck heard the fear in his brother's voice, even as he spoke the words that were supposed to comfort them both.

Ken drew in a long, deep breath and slowly released it. "I'd better get back in there. Want to come with me?"

"Nah. I don't think she wants the bachelor brother-in-law watching her give birth. I'll wait out here. If you need me, you know where I'll be."

"Okay. If you're sure."

"I'm sure. Tell Sara I'm praying for all of you."

Ken nodded, his eyes watery. Then he turned and walked away, disappearing through a pair of doors.

Buck felt like pacing, the way his brother had been doing when he arrived, but he doubted pacing on a scooter would do him any good. So he rolled it to the waiting area and sat on one of the chairs.

CHARITY'S HEART RACED AS THE ELEVATOR CARRIED her upward. Instinct told her to run away, to get out of there. But when the doors opened, she pressed her lips into a tight line and stepped onto the floor, resolved not to let fear or the sins and regrets of the past rule over her.

She found Buck in a waiting area. *Thank You, God.* She wasn't sure resolve would have carried her into the delivery unit itself. Taking the chair next to him, she hesitated, then reached out and patted his shoulder, offering wordless comfort. Then they simply sat in silence, lost in thoughts.

Charity's thoughts took her back ten summers.

The contraction made Charity stop walking. She buckled forward, gasping for breath. Her roommate, Danielle, held on to her arm and kept her from toppling over.

It's too soon. It's too soon.

She straightened. At two in the morning, the hospital was strangely quiet. There were only a few people in the waiting area as she checked in with the nurse. In moments a wheelchair appeared, pushed by a grim-faced orderly, and she was whisked away from her friend and taken into a web of hallways and private elevators.

She hadn't wanted this baby. She'd almost had an abortion. That's what Jon had demanded she do when she'd told him she was pregnant. But she hadn't been able to go through with it. Why, she couldn't say. She'd hated every moment of her baby's life, from conception right up to now. She'd resented the lies she'd had to tell because of it. She'd resented the secrets she'd had to keep. She'd despised the boy—by no stretch of the definition a man—who had done this to her. She'd hated herself even more for allowing that horrid night to happen.

But her ordeal would have been over in another eight or nine weeks. The adoption arrangements had

all been made. With a little creativity in her wardrobe, she had finished the spring semester without
anyone at college knowing she was pregnant. And if
the birth had happened on schedule, she'd expected
to be back in school for the fall semester without anyone the wiser.

Only now she was in labor with a baby whose
chances of survival had dropped considerably. If it
did survive, would the prearranged family still want to
adopt it, especially if it had developmental problems?

*It's your fault this is happening. You hated it, and now
you're being punished.*

The baby was a boy. She'd been told that a few
weeks ago. But she'd never called it "him" or "he."
That would have made it too real. That would have
made it a child who would have a name and a future.
Someone she might learn to love.

As nurses bustled about her, asking questions,
helping her out of her clothes, attaching instruments
of one kind or another, she started to cry. Silent
tears, welling up and then spilling over, streaking her
cheeks. How could she have made such a mess of her
life before she'd turned twenty? How could she—

"It's a boy."

The words broke through Charity's memories, and she
looked up. Ken stood before them, happiness and fear mingling together on his face.

"He's small, but not as small as they expected. Right
at five pounds. All systems seem to be working properly,

but they'll still keep him in NICU for a while. Sara came through everything fine." Ken pulled Buck up from the chair, and the brothers hugged, patting each other on their backs in perfect rhythm. "I've gotta go back in. I'll bring more news when I can."

As his brother hurried away, Buck dropped into the chair, exhaling. "Thank God," he whispered.

"I'm sorry, Charity." The doctor's voice, soft and grim, seemed as real and present as if the physician were speaking now and not a decade ago. *"Baby boy . . . stillborn . . ."*

Suddenly she couldn't breathe. The walls were closing in. The room was too warm. She had to get out. She had to find air. She leapt to her feet and rushed down the wide hallway toward the elevators.

"Charity?" Buck called after her.

She ignored him in her desperate need to escape.

BUCK DIDN'T KNOW WHAT TO DO. SHOULD HE GO after her? The expression on her face the instant before she'd bolted—the pain and utter despair—had been like a knife to his chest. He didn't know why she'd reacted that way. Ken's news had been mostly positive. But something had sent her into flight. Something connected with how she'd reacted back at the house. Buck ached for her and felt a strong need to help her in some way.

It would be crazy to try. They were neighbors for the summer. Friendly acquaintances at most. The last thing he should want was to interfere in her personal life. He didn't need to get entangled in emotions with someone like her. Besides, involving himself would likely give her ideas. He knew how women thought. Charity had told him her plans for the future included marriage. His plans for the future didn't. Whatever had upset her, he should keep his nose out of it.

He *would* keep his nose out of it. No matter how heart-broken and afraid she looked.

Chapter 9

CHARITY DIDN'T KNOW HOW MUCH TIME PASSED before the panic attack faded. It had taken her by complete surprise. Only once before had her fears overwhelmed her to such an uncontrollable point, and that had been years ago when she'd run into Jon Riverton during a visit to Kings Meadow. The loss of the baby had still been fresh, as had Jon's ugly threats.

No, don't think of that again.

Drawing a steadying breath, she rose from the bench and turned toward the entrance of the hospital. She wished she could abandon Buck where he was, leave him to his own resources, but she couldn't. She'd driven him to Boise. She would have to drive him back home again.

But she dreaded what he would say to her.

Moving slowly, trying to bring every thought captive—something she worked hard to achieve on a daily basis—she went into the hospital and returned to the delivery wing. Buck was where she'd left him.

When he saw her, his eyes filled with compassion. "Are you okay?"

"Yes."

"I didn't know what to think when you—"

"I'd rather not talk about it, Buck. Please."

He was silent for several long moments before saying, "All right. We won't."

She could tell he wasn't happy to let it end there.

"We can leave if you're ready," he said after a brief silence. "Ken was out a little while ago. He's planning to stay overnight."

"What about the children?"

"Krista's thirteen already and babysits for others. So they're all right for one night. Their neighbor said she'd be close at hand if needed. We'll figure out what to do the rest of the time when Ken comes home tomorrow."

Charity nodded, taking a moment to process the situation. She loved Sara. She was thankful for the good prognosis for both mother and baby. She was glad the Leonard children had someone to look out for them.

Buck pushed up from the chair and put his knee on the scooter. "We'd better get something to eat before we head home. Is the hospital cafeteria okay or would you rather stop for a hamburger?"

She wasn't hungry. "Here's fine."

"You sure?"

"I'm sure." *Let's just get it over with and get out of here.*

They made their way to the cafeteria. Charity grabbed two trays, putting her food choices on one and what Buck wanted on the other. At the register, he paid for the meals with cash. Then he led the way to a nearby table. Charity slid the trays onto it, thankful that nothing spilled in the process. Her hands weren't completely steady.

Buck must have noticed. He looked ready to ask her again if she was okay, but she sat and picked up her fork, gaze locked on her plate, sending an unmistakable message for him to back off. He got the point.

They ate in silence.

They drove through Kings Meadow as the early-evening sun was throwing long shadows before them. Main Street was quiet.

"Cocoa's gonna be glad to see you," Buck said.

"I know." Her tone was cool, the words clipped.

Mighty frosty in this car. He glanced in her direction and his irritation dissolved. He'd never seen anyone who looked as lost and friendless as Charity Anderson did at this moment. His determination to stay out of her business vanished along with his irritation. He meant to knock down that wall she'd thrown up around herself. Maybe he wouldn't knock it down today. Maybe he wouldn't be able to do it until he got these casts off and felt like himself again. But somehow he would win her trust and find out how he could ease her pain.

At the house, she helped him up the steps, said a quick good-bye, and got back into her car. He watched from behind the screen door until the Lexus pulled away. Then he rolled to the living room and took up his position on the sofa.

But he couldn't stop thinking about Charity.

He got up again and went to the bookcase. On the bottom shelf were his high school yearbooks. He grabbed the one from his senior year and returned once again to the sofa. The side table lamp shed light onto the pages as he began flipping through the book.

High school had been a good time for Buck. Not that he'd been the greatest of students. He'd had to work hard for every decent grade he got. Sports had been his sweet spot. Particularly baseball. He'd loved to rodeo too. Anything to do with horses and the outdoors had made him happy. But baseball was supposed to have been his gateway to the world.

"Let's see about you, Miss Charity Anderson."

He found her photograph and stared at it. It looked like her, but it didn't. Her face looked rounder, her hair a darker shade of blond. Or at least the photo made it look that way. Her expression was intensely serious. He suspected, unlike him, she didn't remember high school as a good time.

She'd changed a lot since then. But who didn't after a dozen years? Neither one of them were kids any longer.

But he couldn't remember seeing or hearing about anything that would have put that broken expression on her face today. It didn't make sense to him either. Most of the time she looked like what she was: a successful, single woman with—What did his mom call it? Oh, yeah.—the world as her oyster. Sure, she'd said she wanted to get married, but also that she didn't have any serious prospects. So today had been about something else.

"What made you bolt, Charity?" He rubbed his thumb over her photo in the yearbook.

He flipped through more pages, trying to remember who'd been her close friends back then. He drew a blank. It seemed to him that she'd spent most of her time with her older sister and her sister's friends. Maybe he could ask Sara, when she was up to it. Although waiting would be difficult. He wanted answers now.

Maybe Ashley knows.

Ashley was in town for a day or two. She tended to know all of the Kings Meadow gossip, despite not living in Kings Meadow. Ken called her a "gossip magnet."

No. Buck wouldn't ask Ashley. It would feel like . . . like he was betraying Charity. Dumb, he supposed, but there it was. He would have to figure this out on his own.

You need to let somebody in, Charity. Might as well be me.

CHARITY LAY ON THE SOFA, A MOVIE PLAYING ON THE television for the company it gave her rather than for entertainment. Cocoa sat on the floor within easy reach. Charity stroked the dog's head while tears streaked her cheeks.

There was a hole in her heart, left by the baby who had never drawn breath, the baby she wished she'd never conceived, the baby she'd wanted to be free of. She'd hated the boy who had used her, laughed at her, and impregnated her. Hated him . . . and feared him. Hated him for what he'd done. Feared him for what he'd promised to do, what he could do, if she ever told the truth to anyone.

She put her fingers to her throat. It was as if hands from

the past were closing around her neck, squeezing off the air from her lungs.

The telephone rang. She ignored it until it went to the answering machine. "Hi. This is Sophie"—It changed from her mom's voice to her dad's—"and Will." Back to her mom. "We aren't available at the moment. Leave a message and we'll get back to you when we can. Thanks."

A beep sounded, followed by a dial tone. No message left.

Her tears dropped onto the sofa. *Splat. Splat. Splat.* What she wouldn't give to be held in her mom's arms right now. What she wouldn't give for a dose of her dad's wisdom.

I don't want to be like this anymore. Why can't I control these thoughts and emotions?

Counseling hadn't helped. She'd tried seeing psychologists several different times in the past.

But you didn't tell any of them the whole truth. How could they help if you weren't completely honest?

Maybe that was one reason why she loved to write novels. Her life, her emotions, were uncontrollable at times. But when she wrote, she was the decider of the fate of her characters. She decided who lived or died. She decided what calamities might befall them and how they would overcome their circumstances. In her story world she could vanquish a villain with a few keystrokes and heal a broken heart with a few well-chosen words.

Real life never worked out that way.

Cocoa put her front paws on the sofa and licked Charity's tear-salted cheek. It made her want to smile, despite the sadness knotting her insides.

The telephone rang again. She listened to the message.

But this time, after the beep, she heard her sister's voice. "Charity, are you there? Pick up, will you?"

She reached for the portable handset. "Hi, Terri."

"What's wrong? You sound like you've been crying."

"No." Charity sat up. "I fell asleep on the couch." The lie came easily to her lips. Terri was the most observant member of the family, and Charity had to be extra careful whenever they talked and especially when they were together. "What's up?"

"I heard about Sara. I was told you and Buck went to Boise to be with Ken at the hospital."

Small-town news rides a fast horse.

"What more can you tell me?" Terri continued.

"Not a lot. Sara's fine, Ken said. They have a son. He's premature and will be in the hospital for a while, but Ken indicated the prognosis is good. Sara and Ken are staying there with the baby. Not sure for how long."

Terri released a deep breath and whispered, "Thank You, Jesus."

Charity felt the threat of tears again and swallowed hard.

"I'm glad you were able to drive Buck so he could be there for his brother. It would've driven him crazy to be far away from his family in a crisis. He's such a stand-up guy."

Strange, wasn't it? That Charity was the one who'd had a crush on Buck back in school, but her sister was the one who knew him well. Although, come to think of it, in high school all Charity had cared about was how cute he was and how all the other girls seemed to like him too.

Having that kind of shallow attraction toward a boy was what had gotten her into trouble.

"Charity, are you listening?"

"Sorry. I got distracted." Not a lie. "Let me turn off the TV." Okay, that was sort of a lie. She grabbed the remote and pressed the Off button so it wouldn't be. "What did you say?"

"Ashley Holloway called me. She's trying to get commitments for the reunion this summer. She said you're going. Is that right? Because if you are, Rick and I will definitely be there."

Charity felt her heart sink. "I thought you were going to be on vacation that weekend."

"We were, but we can move things around on the calendar. Be there, sis. It'll be good for you to see all of your old friends. Generations of friends. Really. You'll have a good time."

"I don't want you to change your vacation."

"No. Listen. I've made up our minds." Terri laughed, and Charity could imagine how she smiled at her husband right then. "We're coming and we'll all go to the reunion together. We'll bring Frankie and stay with you that weekend, and then we'll take off on our vacation when the reunion is over. It's settled. Mark your calendar. No writing while we're there."

"Yes, ma'am." She saluted, even though she couldn't be seen.

Her sister laughed again.

Maybe Terri was right. Maybe it would be good for her to see all of her former classmates and their siblings, parents, spouses, and kids. Maybe isolation from everything and everyone in Kings Meadow hadn't done her any favors through the years.

"Okay, Toot-sweet. You win. It's on my calendar."

"Wonderful." Terri said something to Rick, her voice muffled, likely by a hand over the mouthpiece. Then she came back. "Guess I'll let you get back to your snooze on the couch. Take care, Pipsqueak. Love you."

"Love you too."

Charity ended the call, a sigh slipping through her lips. It wouldn't be as easy as it sounded. How was she to control the unwanted memories? Look what had happened to her today. She needed to overcome, and it was obvious that in order to do so she would need something beyond the self-help books she'd read over the past years. She needed more.

"Come on, Cocoa. Let's take you outside so we can go to bed." She stood. "I'll pretend I'm Scarlett." She feigned her best Southern belle accent. "After all, 'tomorrow is another day.'"

For the first time in hours, she smiled.

Chapter 10

BUCK DIDN'T HAVE ANY REAL OPPORTUNITIES OVER the next week to break through Charity's defenses. Every day, when she came over to exercise one or two of the horses, she asked if he needed her to do anything for him. He tried to think of what that might be, but the truth was he was getting along well. He'd mastered the art of garbage bags over his casts and washing while half in and half out of the shower. He'd become somewhat adept with his left hand. He'd even figured out a way to get outside to the patio on his own, although he hadn't put it into practice yet.

His opportunities to talk seriously with Charity were further diminished by his nieces and nephew. They had come to stay with him so their dad could remain in Boise with their mom and baby brother. Jake played video games on the TV for too many hours each day. The girls spent most of their time talking on the phone with friends or whispering to each other while sitting on the bed in the guest bedroom. But still, their presence in his home was a deterrent. He needed to be alone with Charity if he ever hoped to learn the cause of the pain she obviously wanted to hide from him and everyone.

More casseroles arrived, thanks to the women's ministry at the church. Nobody was starving to death. All the same, Buck wasn't going to buy pasta anytime too soon. He'd had his fill of macaroni in all its different forms.

Ken and Sara returned to Kings Meadow in the evening on the third of July with little Edward James Faulkner Malone—Eddy for short—in his mother's arms. Buck got to give the little guy a kiss on his forehead, but there was no way he was going to hold a baby that tiny. Not with a bum arm. What if he accidentally hit Eddy in the head with his cast? Or worse, dropped him. No, he would wait a couple of months at least. Maybe when Eddy was double his current weight.

Instead, he sat back and watched his brother dote on his wife and new son.

After Ken left with his family, Buck expected to feel a rush of pleasure at the solitude. It didn't happen. In its place came a heightened awareness of a bad case of cabin fever. A trek to the patio, with or without assistance, wasn't going to make it better. He needed a real-live outing, and he knew just where he could find it.

. . .

The next day Grant Nichols picked up Buck half an hour before the parade was due to begin. They were on their way in minutes.

"I really appreciate this," Buck said for the second time as Grant turned his Jeep out of the driveway.

"Glad to help out. Wish I could hang around for the fun, but there's a big do out at the Leonard Ranch tomorrow. I've a lot of preparation to take care of before then."

"How do you like cooking for their guests?"

"I like it. I don't have to stick to a limited menu the way I do at the restaurant. Chet's given me lots of freedom. We try to feed the guests as if they were staying at a five-star hotel."

Buck gave his head a shake. "The whole idea sounded cockeyed crazy when I first heard about it last summer. *Glamping.* But from the looks of it, I was wrong."

"You know, you ought to talk to Chet about leading excursions into the mountains for Ultimate Adventures. They're booked solid through the rest of the summer and into fall, and the guests are partial to trail riding. Bet you could pick up a bunch of work. I'd work for them full-time if I could, but the glamping business is seasonal. Just like your outfitting work. What a life, huh?" He gave a short laugh. "Anyway, Chet's going to need more help soon. Denny Haskins has taken a job in Colorado."

Ordinarily Buck wouldn't give much thought to Grant's suggestion. He liked the independence of working for himself. But this wasn't an ordinary year. He'd kept his clients happy by finding replacement guides for all of the trips booked through July, but he'd still lost momentum. It would take effort to get it back. Chet Leonard's new enterprise might be the right short-term solution to help with his bottom line.

Grant stopped his Jeep near the town park. Crutch, camp chair, cooler, and umbrella marked Buck's spot a short distance away from the sidewalk. The grass was cut short, and he maneuvered the scooter across the hard ground without any problem.

"Anything else I can do to help?" Grant asked.

"Nope. I'm good for the day. Tom Butler said he'll take me home when I've had enough."

Grant tapped index finger to forehead, then returned to his vehicle and drove away.

Buck wasn't ready to sit in the camp chair. He'd had his fill of sitting. He wanted to move around, get some fresh air and a modicum of exercise. So he returned the scooter to the sidewalk and rolled to where a crowd was gathering at the opposite end of the park. Waiting for the parade, no doubt. He joined them.

"Hey, look who's here." Madeline Shaver gave her head a shake, her gaze on the scooter and ankle cast. "Boy, does that bring back memories."

Buck remembered that Madeline, the mother of one of his friends, had broken her leg awhile back. Only hers had required surgery and a much lengthier recovery than his own.

"How much longer have you got?" she asked as if reading his thoughts.

"Not sure, but my last X-ray looked good. Maybe two to three weeks. Won't be any too soon for me."

The woman laughed softly. "I remember feeling the same way."

Sounds of the school's marching band reached their ears and all eyes turned west. Another minute or two and a couple of kids carrying flags rode horses into view. Their mounts pranced in time to the music—or at least it appeared that way. One of the horses was obviously unhappy with the parade duty. It tossed its head and strained against the bit. But the young rider, a girl, remained in control. For some reason the girl made him think of Charity.

For someone who said she hadn't ridden in ages, Charity sat a horse well. Buck knew because he'd watched her whenever she came over to ride. One day she hadn't bothered to saddle a horse. Hadn't bothered with a bridle either. She'd swung up on the horse's bare back, held on to a clump of mane, and cantered the gelding in a wide circle around the acreage. She'd looked happier and more free that day than he'd ever seen.

Made him wish he'd been the cause of that happiness.

I miss spending time with her.

Strange, wasn't it? Added up, they hadn't spent all that many hours together. And yet he missed her company, missed the talks they'd had, missed learning something new about her. There was far more to learn about her than the pain she tried to hide, and he'd like to learn it all.

As if summoned by his thoughts, Charity stepped into view on the opposite side of the street. She wore a loose-fitting white top with spaghetti straps, bright-pink shorts, and flip-flops. Her blond hair was high on her head in a ponytail, and she wore large, dark glasses. She looked adorable, especially when she smiled.

But who was that guy beside her, the one she was talking to? Was he the reason for her smiling appearance? Buck didn't recognize him. He also didn't recognize that tight sensation in his gut. As if he *did* know the guy and didn't like him. Made no sense. Maybe he needed to eat something. It had been awhile since his breakfast of cold cereal.

Half an hour later, the tail end of the parade passed Buck's location, and he turned with the rest of the crowd toward the park and the beginning of the barbecue. He decided to wait until people thinned out over near the grills before he attempted to get a hamburger or hot dog. It might be tricky, maneuvering the scooter down the incline and across that wide stretch of grass.

He rolled on down the sidewalk to where his camp chair awaited him. Once settled, he popped open the top of the small cooler and pulled out a Diet Dr. Pepper. Without the utility of his right hand, he used his teeth to unscrew the top of the plastic bottle. When he looked up, prepared to take his first long drink, he saw Charity walking toward him with a paper plate in hand. That same guy she'd been with earlier kept pace at her side.

"Hi, Buck," she said when she got close enough not to have to shout. "You didn't tell me you were coming. I would have given you a ride into town."

"I didn't decide until last night. A friend came and got me."

"Are your nieces and nephew around?"

"Nope. They went home with their parents last night." Her smile slipped a little. "With the baby?"

"With the baby. He's putting on weight and doing great."

The smile returned, and she held out the paper plate, complete with hamburger, potato salad, and coleslaw. "I brought you some food. Might be a little hard for you to get to the grills and back on your own. I didn't put the works on the burger. This way it won't be quite as messy, one-handed."

"Thanks." He took the plate. "Aren't you eating?"

"Roger and I are going back for ours now. I saw you were alone so thought I'd bring yours over first."

Roger who? He glanced toward the stranger, who had stopped a few steps back.

Charity glanced over her shoulder. "Roger, come here and meet Buck Malone. He lives next door to my parents." She drew the man up beside her. "Buck, this is Roger Bentley. Roger and I used to work in the same firm, before I quit to write full-time. He and his brothers are staying at the Leonard Ranch this week. He didn't remember I was from Kings Meadow until we ran into each other before the parade. Small world, huh?"

"Yeah. Small world." Balancing the paper plate on his thighs, Buck held out his left hand. "Pleased to meet you."

"And you." Roger glanced at the casts on Buck's arm and leg. "A horse do that to you?"

"No. A dog."

Charity laughed. "What Buck didn't say was that the dog who did it was mine."

"Ouch." Roger grinned at Charity.

Buck *really* didn't like the guy.

"We'd better get something to eat ourselves," Charity said. "See you later, Buck."

"Yeah. See you later."

THE FESTIVITIES HAD BEEN LIKE A TONIC FOR Charity. She'd had to force herself to come, but once here, she'd had a great time. It was all so familiar—the people, the parade, the food—and it felt right to be a part of it.

She glanced over her shoulder as she and Roger headed back to the barbecue grills. Buck was right where he'd been, of course, and his gaze followed her. Knowing it caused an odd flutter in her chest.

Since the evening she and Buck had returned from the hospital in Boise, Charity had spent every day doing the same four things—writing her book, analyzing her emotions, taking Cocoa for walks, and riding Buck's horses.

When writing, she'd thought about Buck. A lot. How could she not, since he'd become the inspiration for her hero? She'd thought about the slightly disheveled look of his dark hair. The look that made her want to run her fingers through it. She'd thought about the lazy kind of smile he sometimes wore, when one side of his mouth curved higher than the other side.

When analyzing her emotions, she'd thought about Buck. A lot. He was steady and grounded. So unlike what she'd thought he was. So unlike Charity, who could be knocked off her feet by the slightest breeze. She needed to be more like him.

When walking the dog, she'd thought about Buck—and not just because of the part Cocoa had played in his broken bones. She'd thought about the life he had here in Kings Meadow. Simple. Uncomplicated.

And when riding the horses, she'd thought about . . . nothing. No. Not true. She'd thought about Buck then, too, and she'd imagined what he must look like astride a horse, Stetson shading his eyes, a relaxed grasp on the reins.

Why do I think of him so often? He's just a neighbor. At most a friend.

"Hey, look," Roger said, intruding on her churning thoughts. "There are my brothers."

She followed his gaze to where two men were talking

with three local gals. Mutual flirtation was obvious even from a distance.

"Do you mind if I join them?" Roger continued, eagerness in his voice.

Charity couldn't help but smile, seeing the way he checked out the twenty-something females with his brothers. She didn't mind that he would rather be with them. At one time it would have bothered her. Not today. "No. That's fine. Go ahead. Hope the rest of your stay at the Leonard Ranch is great."

"Thanks. It was good seeing you again, Charity. Take care. Good luck with your books."

With a nod and a wave, she got in a line for one of the grills, exchanging greetings with people she'd known all of her life, answering a few questions about where her parents were now and how they were enjoying their trip abroad, thanking those who complimented her books and shrugging when they asked when the next one would release. But all the while, she felt a tug back toward the edge of the park. Back toward Buck Malone.

"Charity!"

The familiar voice made her spin about. Her eyes quickly found her sister, who hurried toward her, husband and daughter right behind.

"Terri!" They hugged. "I didn't know you were coming."

"Neither did we. We didn't decide until this morning. Threw stuff in the car and here we are. Didn't make the parade, but we won't miss the food or the dancing and fireworks. You don't care if we bunk at the house for a couple of nights?"

"Care? I'd love the company." She tipped her head toward the grills. "I'm after a hamburger. You?"

"We're all famished," Terri replied.

Charity turned and hugged her thirteen-year-old niece, Frankie, who was looking much too grown up since the last time Charity had seen her. Then she hugged her brother-in-law, Rick. In line again and moving closer to the bank of grills, she and Terri hooked arms.

Her sister said, "I heard Sara and the baby are home."

"Yes. Yesterday. Buck just told me."

"Is he here?"

Charity nodded. "Back there, closer to the gazebo. A friend brought him."

"I'll have to say hi after we eat. And commiserate with him for what you and Cocoa did."

Charity elbowed her sister but grinned as she said, "Sure. Whenever you want."

WHEN BUCK HAD CHOSEN THE SPOT TO SET HIS CAMP chair—up a slight incline and overlooking the park, gazebo, and temporary dance floor—he hadn't expected the location to work like a magnet, drawing people to him. He hardly had time to eat his burger before it got cold. Folks kept stopping by, asking how he was doing, wishing him well, passing along tidbits about happenings in Kings Meadow.

After about the fifteenth interruption, he started to wish he'd stayed home. But then, in a rare moment alone, he saw Charity walking toward him for the second time that day, and thoughts of wanting to go home vanished. Especially since that Roger fellow was nowhere in sight. But her sister, Terri, was.

"A nice surprise to see you here," he said to Terri when the two women arrived.

She returned his smile. "I had to come see the damage my sister did to you."

"My dog did the damage," Charity protested as she rolled her eyes. "Not me. Thank you very much."

Terri laughed as she sank to the ground, her gaze still on Buck. "I take it you won't be dancing tonight."

"Not tonight." He enjoyed dancing when he had two good feet, but he didn't think his trusty scooter would serve him well on the dance floor. "Rick come with you?"

"Yes." Terri glanced around the park. "He and Frankie are out there somewhere. They'll find us eventually."

Buck's gaze shifted to the younger Anderson sister. Charity was also seated on the grass by this time. It surprised him, how he noticed everything about her. The mixture of light and dark shades in her hair. The high cheekbones. The deep blue of her eyes. The fullness of her mouth. The nice curves of her slender body. The laugh that was distinctly hers. The way she walked.

Whoa. I wanted to help her. Nothing more. And she doesn't even look like she needs help today.

Right now it seemed everything about her was close to perfect. It seemed—

He looked away, his mouth and throat dry. He grabbed a bottle of water from the cooler, removed the cap, and drank half of it before pausing to draw breath. By that time, others had come over to say hello to Terri and to ask Buck how he was doing.

Suddenly, the more people around, the better, as far as Buck was concerned.

Chapter 11

Freedom!

Buck stood—sans both casts—at the fence and stared across the pasture to where his horses grazed at the far end of the property. A shallow creek ran along the back fence, and trees and shrubs lined its banks, providing shade at this time of day. He longed to slip through the slats of wood and stride out to the horses, maybe even swing up on one of them, but the doctor had told him to take it easy, especially since he was out of the casts earlier than expected. He had been instructed to do exercises to strengthen the muscles and get his flexibility back. Plus he had to wear a splint on his ankle. But until the swelling went down, it would be impossible to get that foot into a boot, so the splint didn't matter much to Buck.

"I've seen much worse swelling," the doctor had told him an hour ago. "It won't be long before it looks normal again." Dr. Frederick had also insisted Buck use a cane for the next week or so. Buck hadn't intended to follow that advice, certain he wouldn't need it and vain enough not to want to look like an old man when out in public. But he had to admit, he was less steady on his feet than he'd expected.

He glanced down at his right wrist, wrapped in an Ace bandage, and began to turn it in small circles, first one way, then the other. No pain, but it had been weakened, like his ankle.

He turned from the fence, and his glance went in the direction of the Anderson home. Since the Fourth of July celebration they'd fallen into an easy routine. She would knock on the door, ask if he needed anything, stand on the stoop and chat with him about nothing in particular, fingers tucked into the back pocket of her jeans. Then she would head out to the pasture and the horses.

Buck liked watching her brush them and pat them. He liked the easy way she talked to them, although he couldn't hear her words. He took surprising pleasure in watching her ride. He also enjoyed looking out the window and watching her throw a ball for Cocoa or playing tug-of-war with a knotted rope. Simply looking at her made him feel good. And when she was out of sight, he missed her. He wanted to be with her.

He glanced down at his right foot, remembering how he'd thought it might be fun to have Charity around while he recuperated. It was supposed to have been a lark. After all, they weren't headed in the same direction. They wanted different things out of life.

Only that didn't feel as true now as it had back at the start.

Keeping an eye on the uneven ground, he headed for the house and a cool glass of iced tea. After that, he would sit down with his calendar and try to get some work done.

Update some records in the computer. Pay a few bills. Balance his checking and saving accounts. All of the paperwork that he'd let slide since his fall.

He was just inside the back door when the telephone rang. It was his brother.

"Hey. I heard you got your casts off early."

"Yeah, the doctor said I'm a fast healer."

"That's great because Sara wants you to come over for dinner. You haven't seen Eddy since we brought him home, and she's dying to show him off to his uncle."

"Are you sure that's not too much for her?"

Ken lowered his voice. "Her mom's doing the cooking. Come on, bro. I'm outnumbered."

Buck laughed.

"Sure. You find it funny. You know I'm fond of Irene, but she's been here almost two weeks. The house seems to be shrinking."

"All right. I'll come. What time?"

"Would now be too soon?"

Buck thought of all the bookkeeping tasks he needed to do, then answered, "Nope. Not too soon. I'll be right over."

"Oh. You can drive? I thought I'd come get you."

"Not a chance. No more chauffeuring for me. I'll be there in ten minutes." He dropped the phone into its cradle, took the keys to his truck in one hand and the cane in the other, and headed outside again.

It felt strange to be behind the wheel after so many weeks of being driven around by his brother and friends. Tom Butler had taken him to and from the clinic that morning. Hopefully it would be Buck's last time to need that kind of help. Ever.

He shoved the clutch to the floor with his left foot, then placed his right foot on the gas pedal, moving it around a bit, testing the up-and-down motion. The splint didn't interfere. Then he checked the brake as well. His ankle felt a little too weak—at least if a fast, hard brake was required—but he could use his left foot in an emergency.

As he pulled out onto the road, he couldn't help himself. He leaned out the window and let out a whoop of joy.

Freedom!

WITH A SIGH, CHARITY CLOSED HER LAPTOP AND rolled her chair back from the desk. When she whirled the chair around, she was surprised to find the light fading outside. She couldn't believe it was that late. Was a storm brewing? She rose and went to the window. No. The sky was clear. A glance at the bedside clock told her it was after nine p.m. No wonder her backside felt numb. She hadn't moved from the chair in several hours.

Cocoa whimpered from the doorway.

Charity turned. "I'm sorry, girl. Need out?"

The dog wagged her tail and did a little dance.

"All right." Charity laughed. "Let's go outside."

As usual, Cocoa didn't wait around for her mistress. She was down the stairs in an instant and stood near the door, waiting for Charity to catch up with her.

"No walk today, girl. It's too late. I'll throw the ball for you instead." She reached for the yellow tennis ball that she kept in a basket near the door.

Cocoa quivered with excitement from the tip of her nose

to the tip of her tail. The moment they were both outside, Charity threw the ball as hard as she could in the direction of Buck's front yard, and the dog took off after it. Charity settled onto the top step of the front porch.

Buck's truck was gone from the side of his house, the spot where it had been ever since the accident. The pickup hadn't been there the last time she'd looked either. She flinched at the thought, not liking that she'd made note of it.

Cocoa brought the ball back and Charity threw it again—in the same direction.

Wasn't it enough that she thought about Buck during the day while she was writing? Lately he had invaded her dreams as well. Which seemed worse—more dangerous—than her old nightmares, as crazy as that sounded.

She was about to throw the ball one more time for Cocoa when the sounds of Buck's truck drew her eyes to the road. He waved at her through the open window of his pickup as he turned into the driveway.

"Sit, Cocoa."

The dog obeyed as Charity rose to her feet.

Buck got out of the truck and, grinning, walked toward her, a cane in one hand.

She couldn't help but return his smile. "Look at you."

"Yeah. Not too shabby."

She glanced toward the pickup and back again. "Must feel good to be able to drive."

"You have no idea."

The twilight dimmed even more, the silence of evening broken by the chirping of crickets and a breeze rustling the leaves on the trees. Cocoa groaned as she lay down.

"Been busy writing today?" Buck asked.

"Yes."

"Going well?"

"Yes. I think so. Better than I expected when I first got here."

"Glad to hear it." He glanced toward the pasture behind his house. "Did you ride today?"

"No, not today." She felt a twinge of regret. With his casts off, he wouldn't need her to exercise his horses any longer. He could do it himself. Look at him. He was on the mend. He would be back to his old life soon. She should get back to hers.

"I had dinner tonight at Ken and Sara's. You should see the baby. It's amazing how much bigger he is already."

There was a catch in her heart, but not as bad as it might have been. "That's wonderful. I'm so glad he's doing well."

He looked at her, and she was glad for the failing light, lest he see too much.

"I . . . uh . . ." She pointed at his leg. "I'd better not keep you standing here."

"I'm all right." But he took a step back from her.

"It's good to see you out and about, Buck. Really it is."

"Thanks." He started to turn, then stopped. "You're still welcome to ride whenever you want."

His words had a wonderful effect upon her, and she smiled her thanks.

"Oh. Almost forgot. Sara said when I saw you to say she's up for visitors and she hopes you'll come to see her and the baby soon."

Charity's earlier calm evaporated. With effort, she forced the smile to remain in place. "I will. I'll go over soon."

Chapter 12

The following Monday, mindful of Grant's suggestion about possible work, Buck drove to the Leonard Ranch north of Kings Meadow. The place had been in Chet Leonard's family since the 1860s, and cattle had covered their land for close to a hundred years. But around the end of World War II, the Leonards had begun the switch to raising quarter horses. Lots of rodeo champions had come from the Leonard Ranch in the years since. Fine working stock too.

Then a year ago, they'd started renting out cabins to guests. Not a dude ranch in the usual way, from what he'd heard, but near enough. *Glamping*, they called it. Short for *glamorous camping*. The name alone made him shake his head.

When he got to the ranch, Buck saw Chet working with a young horse in a corral near the barn. He parked his truck and got out, glad he could manage walking without the cane. It wouldn't feel right to need it when he was applying for work. He went to the corral, his gait a bit choppy but not bad.

Chet met him at the fence. "Hey, Buck. Glad to see you up and around. How are you?"

"I'm good, thanks." He glanced toward the horse in the corral. "Fine-looking colt you've got there."

"Yeah, he is. We're going to keep him, I think, for Kimberly. He's got such an easy temperament, even as young as he is." Chet opened the gate and stepped out. After closing it behind him, he removed his hat and swept his shirtsleeve across his forehead. "Whew. Sure is hot for this early in the day."

Buck nodded. "Sure is."

"So what brings you out our way? You in the market for another horse?"

"Not this year."

Chet nodded and appeared to be waiting for Buck to answer his first question.

Buck drew a quick breath. "Grant Nichols told me you might be looking for someone to take your guests on trail rides. If you are, I'm interested."

Chet's eyes widened. "You are?"

"Yeah. I had to give away a lot of business this summer, and I'm not real sure when I'll be back to full strength." He gave a slight shrug. "I figured taking your guests on trail rides would be something I could do until I'm up for the more strenuous trips into the back country."

"We'd love to have you, Buck. In fact, if I could talk you into it, I'd bring you on for the whole season." Chet laid a hand on Buck's shoulder. "Come into the office, and we'll talk details."

Relief flooded through Buck. This was an answer to prayer.

The two men headed across the barnyard, Chet shortening his stride to accommodate Buck's slower pace. A few minutes later, they entered the single-level cottage that had been transformed into the offices of Leonard Ranch Ultimate Adventures. They were met by Kimberly, Chet's wife of less than a year.

"You remember Buck Malone," Chet said to her. "He's going to lead trail rides for our guests."

Kimberly grinned. "That's wonderful news." She got up from the desk and went to stand by her husband, putting an arm around Chet's waist while still looking at Buck. "I'll bet if you wanted, you could get some orders for your saddles too. I can't tell you how often someone comments on the one Chet had you make for me." Her eyes, filled with love, lifted to meet Chet's gaze.

Buck felt as if he'd intruded on an intimate moment between the pair. He looked away from them, but not before he saw Chet lean down to kiss his wife. He was startled by the envy that shot through him. Startled even more when he pictured himself kissing Charity, holding her close, staring down into her eyes in the exact same way.

Chet cleared his throat. "Come with me, Buck." He led the way into what had once been the bedroom of the cottage. Several filing cabinets, two tall bookcases, a printer on a rolling stand, and a large desk with a computer monitor and keyboard on it took up most of the space. Chet motioned for Buck to sit in one of the chairs near a window while he sat in the one behind the desk. He clicked on the keyboard to awaken the computer and then opened a program on the screen.

Buck had a lot of respect for Chet Leonard. That respect

increased as the two men talked business for the next half hour. They settled quickly upon fair compensation for guiding guests on trail rides. But that wasn't where Chet left it. He had ideas about how they could utilize Buck's expertise to profit them both. By the time they were finished, Buck felt a new confidence. Even if his ankle and wrist weren't up to the task of taking groups into the wilderness area this season, it wouldn't be the ruination of him.

Chet rose from his chair. "Let's drive out to one of the guest cabins so you can get an idea of what we're doing. You've got time, right?"

"Sure." Buck stood. "Time's what I have the most of right now."

Kimberly was on the phone when the two men reentered the front office of the cottage. She wiggled her fingers at Chet. He mouthed that he'd be back soon. She nodded.

"You're a lucky man," Buck said when they were outside again.

Chet smiled. "I'm blessed. No doubt about it."

Chet and Buck got into a big black truck and followed a dirt road north, the fenced pastureland on their right. The mountains drew closer until finally they reached their destination. There, in a cluster of trees, Buck saw a cabin with a couple of large, white-canvas tents nearby.

"It used to be one of the ranch's line shacks from the late 1800s." Chet cut the engine. "Back in the days when those were needed. We did quite a bit of remodeling on the inside but tried to leave it rustic on the outside." He pointed toward the tents. "Large families or groups spill over into those. Come on. I'll show you around."

It wasn't until they'd walked closer to the cabin that Buck saw, off to the right, a covered concrete slab with some work-tables, a large gas grill, a couple of ovens, and a big stovetop with six burners. A sink meant there was running water, and lights overhead meant electricity.

Chet saw the direction of Buck's gaze. "That's where Grant prepares the gourmet meals for our guests. The boys and I manage to serve up a decent breakfast, but we book Grant for most lunches and all of the dinners."

"He likes working out here. He told me so."

Chet gave Buck the rest of what he called the five-cent tour, filling in with amusing stories about some of their experiences as they'd gotten Ultimate Adventures up and running. By the time they were finished and on their way back to the ranch complex, Buck knew he'd made the right decision to drive out to the Leonard place that day.

It might turn out to be a far better summer than expected.

HOLDING A BOX WRAPPED IN IRIDESCENT PAPER IN the crook of her left arm, Charity rang the doorbell. Her stomach churned as she waited. But before she could chicken out, the door opened, revealing a woman Charity had never met before. She didn't have to wonder if she was Sara's mother. There was a striking resemblance between the two.

"Hello," the woman said, her expression friendly. "You must be here to see Sara. I'm her mother, Irene Dover."

"A pleasure to meet you, Mrs. Dover. I'm Charity Anderson."

Irene's eyes widened. "You're the famous author."

"Hardly famous," Charity answered, always uncomfortable when someone said that.

"Come in. Come in." Irene opened the door as far as it would go. "You cannot imagine how excited I am to meet you. Sara sent me your first novel, and I've been hooked ever since. When will your next one be out? Will it be another book in the Lancer series?"

Before Charity could reply, Sara called a greeting from the room at the top of the stairs. "Charity, is that you? Come on up. I'm just about to feed Eddy."

"It's me. I'll be right there." She glanced at Irene. "Excuse me, Mrs. Dover."

"Go on with you. We'll talk later."

"Okay." She hurried up the stairs and into the master bedroom.

Sara was seated in a rocking chair, the baby hidden beneath a blanket draped over Sara's shoulder. Charity heard suckling noises as she settled onto the hope chest at the foot of the bed. Her lungs contracted at the sound.

Breathe. Just breathe.

This was the first time Charity had been anywhere close to a newborn in ten years. She was the friend who sent flowers for the mother and a gift for the baby. She had them delivered along with a nice card. She never visited the hospital before or after a birth. She never called upon a new mother at home, never asked to hold an infant. Had she been fooling herself? Maybe she hadn't the instincts needed to be a mother. Maybe when she thought about the future, about marriage and a family, she was kidding herself. Maybe God didn't want her to have either of them.

Do You, Lord?

"Eddy nurses often," Sara said, breaking into Charity's thoughts.

"Eddy, huh?"

Sara nodded. "We named him for my dad. Edward James Faulkner Malone."

"That's a mouthful." Charity laughed softly—and felt better because of it.

Her gaze moved to the many photos hanging on the wall behind her friend. Some were of Sara as a girl, but most were of the family she'd made with Ken. It was a good family too. A happy family.

Sara had been twelve years old when she moved to Kings Meadow with her father and new stepmother. Sara and Terri had become inseparable in no time at all. Which meant, over time, Charity had become friends with Sara too—once she was no longer considered the pesky little sister.

As far as Charity knew, this was the first time Sara's mother had come to Kings Meadow to see her daughter. She'd missed Sara and Ken's wedding for some reason and hadn't come for the births of her first three grandchildren either. Instead, every year like clockwork, airline tickets arrived for the entire family to fly down to southern California where Irene Dover lived. Charity wondered what had made the difference this time, but she wouldn't ask. If Sara wanted her to know, she would volunteer the information.

"Four kids," Charity said instead, bringing her eyes back to Sara. "Can't believe it. Seems like only yesterday we were kids ourselves."

"I know. And it *was* only yesterday that we were kids."

Sara started the chair rocking gently. "It was good to see Terri over the Fourth. Wish she could have stayed longer."

"Me too."

"You must be glad Buck's out of his casts. He said you did a lot for him."

"Not really. It didn't take him long to learn how to cope."

"Hmm. Not sure I believe you."

"It's true. And even when I did help, he wasn't a demanding patient."

Sara tipped her head a little to one side, seeming to study Charity. "No, he isn't the demanding sort. Always gives more than he takes. I'd love it if he'd meet somebody special to marry. I hate to see him alone all the time."

Charity got up from the chest and walked to the window. She pushed the curtain aside and stared down at the large backyard. It was littered with signs of children—a swing set, a sandbox, bicycles, a tree house. "He told me he doesn't plan to marry."

"He's told us the same thing. I even understand why he says it. But meeting the right woman would make all the difference in the world."

"From what I hear, he's dated all of the single girls within fifty miles of Kings Meadow."

Sara laughed. "That's a slight exaggeration. But yes, he's enjoyed the company of women without any hint of settling down. Although, come to think of it, he didn't seem to do much dating in the last year."

"That must explain why there wasn't a parade of women at his house while he was laid up." She faced her friend again. "Maybe there isn't a right woman for him."

"Maybe." Sara shrugged. "But I hope you're wrong. He would make a great husband and father." Her friend paused for a few moments before asking, "What about you, Charity? Anyone special in your life?"

"No." For an instant, she thought of Nathan. Then she pictured Buck. Nathan lived in the fast lane. Buck didn't even know where the fast lane was. But they had one thing in common: they were both confirmed bachelors and would never be a special someone to her.

"I think Eddy's ready to meet you now." Sara pulled the blanket from her shoulder, revealing the infant in her arms.

Charity's heart began to hammer again as she forced herself to take a couple of steps toward Sara and Eddy.

"Do you want to hold him?"

"No," Charity answered immediately. She took a breath and tried to act casual. "No, I'd better not. He's so little." Sara's eyes were filled with questions. To Charity's relief, she didn't ask them. "I'm afraid I'll drop him," she added quickly as she moved to stand behind the rocking chair. There, she could look down at the baby and be hidden from his mother's inquiring gaze. "He's beautiful, Sara."

"Isn't he? Our little miracle from God."

Tears welled in Charity's eyes. She wanted a miracle, too, she realized. She wanted a chance to do things right. Would God give it to her after all her sinful choices? She'd asked for forgiveness. She'd been forgiven. But did that change the consequences for what she'd done?

And could she ever forgive herself?

Chapter 13

How does a woman know she's in love?

Charity wrote in her plot journal four days later.

Is it just an emotion? Or is it something more, something deeper, than that? How can anyone be sure they have met the one? Is there just one? What does my heroine believe about it? Moon. June. Swoon.

She stopped writing and stared off into space. Was she even working on her characters or plot now? Or was she writing about herself?

What do I believe about love?

Charity hadn't ever been in love. Not really.

In high school, there'd been a secret crush on Buck. Not love. Hormones.

In college, after the experience with Jon, after she lost the baby, she'd returned to the party scene, this time as a place to forget. Although alcohol was always around, she'd never allowed herself to become drunk. She'd feared that loss of control ever happening again. She'd gone out with different boys, hoping for love but fearing any intimacies. Even holding hands had made her want to flee. And above all else, she'd never let any of them see the real Charity.

Many years later, after many men, many dates, many close calls, there had been Nathan. Fun-loving, successful, live-life-to-the-fullest Nathan. She'd wanted to love him, tried to love him.

Again she wrote, not caring that it was no longer about her novel.

Maybe something's wrong with me. Am I incapable of loving someone in that deep way? The way Mom and Dad love each other. The way Terri and Rick or Sara and Ken love each other. And am I unlovable too?

She stopped again and closed her eyes. She rolled the questions around, looking at them with what she hoped was an unbiased perspective. "I'm not unlovable," she determined after a lengthy stillness. "And I'm not incapable. I can love someone. Really love someone. But it must be someone who loves me too."

She thought about the romance novels she'd been reading in order to understand the genre better. Then she thought about the story she was writing, about the roadblocks to love she'd thrown up in the paths of her hero and heroine. And then she realized how very much she wanted the characters to fall in love and find their future together. Not simply to satisfy readers. She wanted it to happen to satisfy herself. She *needed* to see it happen in the pages of her story. She wanted to believe in it. Believe in it way down deep inside.

Through the kitchen window—open to a lovely morning breeze—she heard Cocoa bark a greeting, followed a moment later by the deeper rumble of a man's voice. Not close enough to hear the precise words but close enough to know it was Buck who spoke to the dog. Unable to stop herself—not even wanting to stop—she left the leather-bound journal and gel pen on the table, got up from the chair, and walked to the back door, stopping on the stoop.

Buck was leaning over the fence to stroke and scratch Cocoa, who sat in the grass before him. The dog responded with a few happy slaps of her tail against the ground. Buck straightened, and his gaze went straight to where Charity stood. "Hey. Good morning." He bumped the brim of his hat with his knuckles, pushing it higher on his forehead.

"Morning, Buck."

He opened the gate and strode toward her, Cocoa at his side. He looked good. Real good. Cowboy-hero material for sure.

You'd look rather yummy on a book cover. Heat rushed into her cheeks, and a delicious sensation tumbled in her stomach. *Maybe I've been reading too many romances.*

"How are you?" he asked, either not seeing or ignoring her blush.

"Good. Busy." There was something different about him.

What was it? "You've got both your boots on!" she blurted when she figured out what it was.

"Yep." He grinned. "Today's the first time. Took some hard pulling, but I got it on. Just hope I won't have to cut it off when the day's over."

"I hope so too."

He tilted his head back, removing the shade from his eyes. "I'm going for a ride up in the hills and wondered if you'd like to go with me."

"Oh, I don't—"

"Come on, Charity. You'd enjoy yourself, and the fresh air would do you good. You've been cooped up working for days. I've hardly seen you go outside. You haven't even come over to ride."

A frisson of pleasure whirled in her stomach at the discovery that he'd been watching for her. "I wasn't sure you'd want me to keep riding, now that you're able."

"Sure, I want you to. I've still got six horses that aren't doing the work they're used to. And you still like to ride. Right?"

She nodded.

"Then come with me. This'll be my first time up in the mountains since getting my casts off. Probably better I have someone with me. You know, in case my ankle gives out or something."

Buck's ankle wouldn't give out on him. She would bet good money on that.

"Please come." He gave her one of those slow grins of his.

When had she become helpless against that smile? And she couldn't refuse him. She wanted to go. She wanted to ride in the mountains like she used to, and if she was honest, she wanted the ride to be with Buck.

"All right," she answered at last. "I'll need a few minutes to change my clothes."

"No rush. I've still got to load the horses in the trailer. Come on over when you're ready." He reached down to pat the dog's head again. "Bring Cocoa. She'll have a good time too."

Mom would say I need my head examined. She turned and reentered the house, hurrying up the stairs to the bedroom. *I should be writing, not riding.* She removed her shorts and pulled on jeans, socks, and boots. *But maybe I'll learn something I need to know while we're out there. Something my story needs. That would be a good thing. A productive thing.*

Hair in a ponytail, she placed a baseball cap on her head and pulled her hair through the opening in the back. *A citified cowgirl, if ever there was one*, she thought as she looked at her reflection. But it was the only hat she owned. And besides, she'd never been a real cowgirl. No one would expect her to own a proper cowboy hat.

Before leaving her room, she sprayed sunscreen on her exposed skin, adding an extra dose to her fingertips that she then spread across her nose.

By the time she exited the house, Buck was loading the second horse into the trailer attached to his truck. Cocoa lay in the shade, observing the activity as if bemused by it all, but she didn't remain there for long. She was up on all fours the instant Charity opened the passenger door of the truck.

"Is it okay for Cocoa to ride in the cab?" she asked. "She's never ridden in the bed of a truck before."

"Sure," came the reply from behind the trailer.

Charity stepped to one side. "Come on, girl."

The dog flew into the cab as if she'd been riding in this truck her whole life. Feeling light in spirit, Charity followed. The trailer door creaked closed, and she heard the bolt slide into place, locking it. Moments later, Buck got in behind the wheel.

"I've needed to do this, Charity. Never has been a summer when I've been out of the saddle this long. Not as far back as I can remember. Even in the winter I spend time with my horses and ride whenever weather permits." He turned the key, and the engine rumbled to life. "I thought we'd ride up to McHenry's Sluice. That ought to make it about the right length of ride." He steered the truck out to the road and turned left. "When was the last time you were up that way?"

"Hmm. Probably when I was twelve. The Girl Scouts had a campout up near the cabin." The memory—a happy one—made her smile. The girls and their leaders had been sound asleep when one of the horses got loose and started walking away, stepping over sleeping bags and skirting the campfire. It had caused quite a commotion.

Buck drove to a public parking area in the outermost curve of the valley. Years ago, the county had cleared and leveled the ground, then covered it with dirt and gravel. Ever since, vehicles could be found in this lot during all seasons of the year. Hunters. Snowmobilers. Cross-country skiers. Trail riders. Hikers. Mountain bikers. But for some reason the area was empty of trucks and trailers when Buck and Charity arrived.

Buck parked his pickup near a tall pine tree that would offer the cab some shade later in the afternoon. He and Charity got out, Cocoa following Buck out the driver's side door. They unloaded the horses as if they'd been doing it together for years and were both silent as they began to saddle up their respective mounts. Charity found it a comfortable silence. Did Buck feel the same?

She glanced over the seat of the saddle in his direction. There was something graceful about the way he moved. Graceful, yet masculine at the same time. And watching him brought that fluttering sensation back into her belly.

She lowered her gaze to the cinch and tried to concentrate on the task at hand, not the man standing a short distance away.

BUCK HAD BEEN STRETCHING THE TRUTH, TRYING to convince Charity that he might need help, wanting her to think something could go amiss with his wrist or ankle. Sure, neither were up to full strength or mobility, but he was strong and mobile enough for the intended ride. Still, he would have said close to anything just so she would agree to come along with him. He'd wanted her company that much. He'd wanted it even though he probably shouldn't.

He liked her even though he probably shouldn't.

She wanted marriage. He didn't.

She lived in the city. He was a country boy.

She drove a Lexus. He drove an old beater truck.

She was obviously used to the finer things. He was content with the simple.

He would be foolish to let his feelings go beyond what he might experience for any neighbor. Casual friendship at most.

But when he glanced at Charity as they rode side by side along an old logging road, he knew he'd begun to want something more than friendship. It wasn't because she was beautiful—though she was. It was more than that. She intrigued him. Sometimes she confused him. And always he found pleasure in being with her, even when neither of them said a word.

She turned her head and caught him watching her. "What?" She rubbed her upper lip. "Do I have something on my face?"

"No." He chuckled. "I was enjoying the beauty of nature."

Charity blushed a lovely shade of pink. It was clear she'd understood his meaning.

With perfectly bad timing, Cocoa began to bark in excitement. Buck tightened his grip on the reins. "Easy, boy," he said to the horse.

Cocoa kept right on barking.

"What do you see?" Buck and Charity asked in union.

That surprised them more than the canine commotion, and—once again in unison—they laughed.

"All right, Cocoa." Charity motioned with her hand. "Free."

The dog crashed through the underbrush, chasing something Buck couldn't see. He hoped it was a deer and not a bear, cougar, or skunk. All were possibilities.

Charity must have had a similar thought. Her expression grew worried. "You don't think she'll get into trouble, do you?"

"You never know. Maybe you should call her back. Just to be on the safe side."

Charity pursed her lips, and the whistle that came forth caused the horses to jerk up their heads in alarm. Cocoa reappeared out of the forest a few moments later, tongue hanging out and looking as if she was extremely pleased with herself.

"Who taught you to do that?" Buck asked Charity.

"Do what?"

"You know what I mean. That whistle. You made my ears bleed." He pressed a hand to the side of his head.

She grinned. "Nobody taught me. I've always been able to do it. Ever since I was a kid." She turned her gaze back to the road. "You should hear it when I use my fingers."

Buck laughed again. One more reason to be intrigued. Charity Anderson could look as pretty and feminine as possible one moment—complete with sky-high heels—and then whistle like a foreman in a sawmill the next.

They rode in silence for a short while, Cocoa staying a couple of yards ahead of the horses, as if she knew where they were going. Maybe she did.

When the turnoff came into view, Buck pointed to it. "We'll take that trail there on the left. We'll have to go single file for a while. The trail's narrow. Why don't you take the lead?"

"Great. That'll let me take better pictures of what's up ahead of us." She held up a small camera, not much bigger than the palm of her hand.

Buck didn't blame her for wanting to take photographs. The time of day was just right for it, sunlight slanting through the trees at the perfect angle. Gold shades mingling with greens. Light chasing dark. Occasional glimpses of rugged mountain peaks in the distance.

But there were things about the area that couldn't be captured in a photograph. The breeze that felt cool upon the skin. The sounds of chipmunks scolding from tree limbs and a woodpecker's *tap-tap-tap* in a tree deep in the forest. The air that was scented with pine. Even the dust the horses' hooves stirred up smelled good to Buck.

He silently thanked the Lord for letting him grow up in Kings Meadow, for letting him know these mountains like the back of his hand. He belonged here. It was as much a part of him as the color of his eyes and hair.

Charity twisted in the saddle and snapped a picture of him, then grinned before facing forward again. "Thanks, Buck," she called back to him.

"For what?"

"For asking me to join you today."

"My pleasure."

More than you know.

EVERY KID WHO'D EVER ATTENDED SCHOOL IN KINGS Meadow knew the story of Zeb McHenry. How he'd arrived in what would soon become Idaho Territory. That was in 1862, the first summer of the Boise Basin gold rush. How he'd searched for gold in one of the streams in the mountains to the east and north of Kings Meadow. How he'd fought off claim jumpers. How he'd survived several brutal winters while living in a small, drafty log cabin. How he'd used pans and picks, shovels and sluice boxes, and by the time he left these mountains three years later, how he'd made his fortune.

The remains of McHenry's cabin and one of his sluice boxes were near a popular trail used by hikers, mountain bikers, and horseback riders. From there, adventurers could continue on to higher, more rugged terrain or they could circle back on one of several different trails to the valley below.

Charity spotted the familiar clearing through the trees and snapped a few quick photos before dropping the camera into her shirt pocket. Cocoa made a beeline to the creek and stood right in the middle of the rushing water, lapping it up with her tongue.

Buck and Charity dismounted and let the horses drink, too, while they took sips from their canteens.

About forty feet from the creek and up a gentle slope, McHenry's cabin, most of its roof caved in decades ago, stood in a copse of trees. Although she'd seen the small one-room shack numerous times as a kid, she felt drawn to have a closer look. She tied her horse to a tree limb and then walked to the cabin.

Without a door—also missing for decades—the cabin had become a den for forest creatures. The dirt floor was covered with dried leaves and dead pine needles. A hole in the wall showed where a pipe had once carried away smoke from the fire, but scavengers had taken the stove long ago. When she peered inside, Charity was surprised by how tiny it truly was. How had Zeb McHenry lived in that confined space for months at a time without going stark-raving mad? She tried to imagine living like that and shuddered.

"Feeling claustrophobic?" Buck asked when he stepped to her side.

"How did you know?"

"It's written all over your face." He grinned.

Could he read her that easily? As before, it made her uncomfortable to think he could. She turned away, took her camera, and snapped more photos.

Down at the creek, Cocoa had started to chase something in the water. Perhaps a fish or a frog. Whatever it was, it had the dog jumping and barking and splashing. Her smile reappeared as she took pictures of Cocoa.

"Shall we eat?" Buck asked from behind her.

"Sure."

They returned to the horses. Charity freed a blanket that was tied behind her saddle while Buck retrieved sandwiches and cookies from his saddlebags. Then they carried the items to a place in the shade.

Charity hadn't realized how hungry she was until she took her first bite. "Mmm." She closed her eyes and savored the peanut butter and jelly as if the sandwich were a gourmet meal. "Glad you thought of this." When she opened her eyes again, she found Buck smiling at her. It made her feel breathless and a little exposed. She wished he couldn't do that to her with such ease.

As if taking pity on her, he asked, "What have you heard from your parents lately?"

It was a question she'd grown used to answering. "They're in Tuscany now. Mom wishes they could buy a villa and vineyard and go stay there every summer. At least, that's what Dad says." She took a few sips from her canteen and then stared upward through the swaying ponderosa pines. "I think she's watched *Under a Tuscan Sun* one too many times."

"Don't think I've seen that one."

"Well, maybe it's more of a chick flick, but I think you'd like it." She looked at Buck again. "I'm glad they're having such a good time. They really sacrificed to come up with the money to pay for it. I don't remember a time when they didn't talk about spending an entire summer in Europe, but I'd stopped believing they would actually do it. It would be awful if they went and it wasn't everything they wanted it to be."

"Yeah, that would be bad."

Charity finished her sandwich and washed it down with more water before asking, "Do you bring people up here very often?"

"No, not often. I've hardly ever done day trips. Mostly I guide folks into one of the wilderness areas. Frank Church River of No Return is where I go the most. Occasionally I lead a group as far up as the Selway-Bitterroot or down to the Owyhee River. It all depends on the group and the length of the trip they want. Level of expertise matters too." He shrugged. "Looks like I'm going to be doing more trail rides the rest of this season. Chet Leonard's hired me to take care of his guests. The ones who want to go riding, that is."

"Really? I hadn't heard."

He shrugged again. "It'll be a different kind of work from what I'm used to. You know, being home most nights. But I'm thankful for it."

There was such an ease about Buck Malone. A kind of centeredness that she'd made note of before. He was comfortable in his own skin, her dad would say. It was a rare trait, and one she had to admire. Buck took life as it came—or at least seemed to.

She envied him that ability.

Chapter 14

WHEN THEY LEFT THE CLEARING NEAR McHENRY'S cabin, Buck led the way. He chose a trail that was steeper at the beginning, but that opened up after only a quarter mile, allowing him to fall back and ride beside Charity from then on. The more time he had beside her, the better, he'd decided.

While she might have been content to ride in silence, Buck wanted to keep her talking. It was more than liking the sound of her voice. As much as he'd learned about her over the summer, he hadn't learned enough. He wanted to know more. And so he asked her a question. Something about her writing to start with. When she reached the end of her answer and fell silent, he asked her something else. Whatever popped into his head. He had no agenda beyond knowing her better.

Finally, after close to an hour, she reined in and gave him a hard look. "Enough with the Twenty Questions, Mr. Malone."

For a moment he thought he'd irritated her, but then he saw the smile tugging at the corners of her mouth. He raised his hands, palms up, in a I-couldn't-help-myself shrug.

A little roll of her eyes said she didn't believe him.

They nudged their mounts forward.

"Your turn," she said.

"My turn for what?"

"Don't pretend ignorance. I don't believe you."

Why did he feel so good? He couldn't figure it out. He was almost euphoric.

"Tell me something about yourself that I don't know."

"Something you don't know. Hmm." He rubbed his jaw between thumb and index finger. "I'm kind of an open book. Not sure what that would be."

"All right. Answer this: why didn't you go on to college like everybody expected? I know you said it just didn't work out, but there must be more to it than that."

He shook his head slowly. "You knew my dad died, right?"

"Two or three years after graduation, wasn't it?"

"Two years after, and that whole two years I watched my dad die by degrees. It was tough, helping Mom take care of him, seeing him fight so hard even when there was little hope. Mom couldn't have taken care of him alone. Not physically or emotionally. And even if she'd been strong enough, I couldn't have gone to college. The scholarship wouldn't have paid for everything. What money there was left after the medical bills needed to go to Ken so he could get his master's degree. He was so close to it by the time Dad passed. Plus Ken was married with kids. He had a lot on his plate."

He fell silent for a short while. She didn't intrude on his thoughts.

"It took a long time to dig out of the medical debt. The last of it was paid off when Mom sold the house. Then she moved to live with her sister in Arizona. By that time I was working for the outfitter and discovered how much I liked it."

When he glanced at Charity again, he saw surprise in her eyes.

"I can't believe I didn't know all of that," she said softly, her gaze shifting toward a break in the trees. "I suppose I was too preoccupied with my own life to listen if anybody tried to tell me."

There it was again, that flicker of pain and sadness. Buck hadn't seen it since the day of Eddy's birth, and he'd begun to wonder if it had been a fluke. The times he'd seen her since then, she'd seemed in good spirits.

"I'm sorry, Buck. I should have known how difficult it was for you."

"It's okay, Charity. You weren't around, and I've never talked about it much. Probably plenty more folks than you don't know how it was either."

She released a soft sigh, then repeated, "I'm sorry, Buck."

IT WAS UNPLEASANT, CATCHING A GLIMPSE OF YET another less than noble trait in herself. Buck had been kind, offering her an excuse for her ignorance, but the truth was she'd paid little attention to the trials and tribulations of others for far too long. She'd ignored even those closest to her. Maybe she hadn't been a close friend of Buck's, but someone—most likely her own mother or sister—must have shared some of that news about Buck and his family. But Charity hadn't been listening.

They continued down the mountainside, silence surrounding them at last. Even Cocoa grew quiet, trotting along nearby, no longer looking for small game to stir from the underbrush. Wondering if she'd spoiled the day for Buck, Charity looked over at him. He didn't look upset or troubled. Either he wasn't or he was good at hiding it.

As the pine trees began to thin, Buck pointed off to the south. "Look. There's the backside of the Riverton estate."

Her gaze followed his outstretched arm. She could see the tall, wrought-iron fence and brick posts. Ponderosa pines mostly obscured the house beyond the fence.

"Too bad about Jon."

Charity's throat tightened, but she managed to ask, "What do you mean?"

"He lived large and crashed hard."

"Are the two of you still friends?" She held her breath as she waited for the answer.

"Can't say that we are." Buck frowned. "Not since high school. Jon took a path that I wasn't willing to walk down, and he didn't have time for anyone who didn't want to live and think the same way. After he came home from college, I saw a smallness, a meanness, in him that I didn't recognize when we were younger. Booze and drugs only made it worse, and he was into both. As long as Sinclair was alive, he managed to keep his son a little in check. Once the old man passed, it was a fast slide downhill for Jon. He managed to lose everything his father spent a lifetime building."

A shudder passed through Charity. She remembered the meanness. She'd seen it up close.

"I pray for him when I remember to," Buck added, his voice low.

Pray for Jon. That voice in her heart made her breath catch again. *Pray for him.*

Never. She could never pray for him. Not after what he'd done to her. Not after what he'd taken from her. If not for him—

"Charity?" Buck's hand closed around her horse's reins, stopping him. "What's wrong?"

She shook her head, feeling as though her throat were caught in a vise.

"You can trust me, you know. I'm your . . . friend."

My friend. It felt good to hear him say that.

"I'd like to help if I could. Even if it's only listening."

She met his gaze and shook her head a second time, unable to speak. The secret was lodged too deep inside. A decade of silence had sealed it there.

"Okay." He let go of the reins. "But remember, I'm here if you need me."

If he didn't stop being nice and sensitive and kind, she was going to burst into tears. She clucked to her horse and continued down the trail.

BUCK WASN'T ANYBODY'S FOOL. HE'D NOTICED THE change that came over her when she'd seen the Riverton estate. Her face had gone white, then flushed. He'd heard the difference in her voice when she'd asked about Jon. Two plus two always made four. And Jon plus a girl? All the way back to high school, that combination had meant trouble.

What did he do to you?

Buck wanted to know the answer . . . and dreaded getting one. Both. Equally. At the same moment. But she would have to tell him in her own time and in her own way. *If* she ever told him.

He nudged his horse and caught up with her. "We'll take that cutoff to the left," he said.

That hadn't been his original plan, but the alternate trail would get them out of sight of the Riverton estate faster. That's what was important to him now. He just wanted to take care of Charity.

Take care of Charity.

Not that long ago, Buck had been determined to look out for number one and only number one. So why did taking care of Charity suddenly sound so good to him?

He wasn't sure he wanted to know that answer either. Because if he acknowledged it, everything would change—including Buck himself.

Chapter 15

CHARITY AWAKENED SLOWLY THE NEXT MORNING TO find sunlight pouring through the curtains of the bedroom window. She hadn't slept this late or this soundly in ages. Odd, wasn't it? That she would sleep so well despite the anxiety she'd felt after she and Buck had come near the Riverton estate.

"You can trust me, you know. I'm your . . . friend."

She pulled the pillow over her face, letting Buck's words echo in her memory again and again, savoring the pleasure it gave her. A person could never have too many friends. Too many *true* friends. And she knew without doubt that Buck's would be the true kind of friendship. She would be thankful for it even after she returned home and her life got back to normal.

Back to normal.

She pushed the pillow aside and sat on the side of the bed.

Back to normal.

The last time she'd spoken to her contractor, everything had been going well. And right now the same could be said for her book. With any luck, both would be finished in another five to six weeks. When she'd arrived in Kings Meadow, staying here for the summer had felt like a prison sentence. Now—

The telephone rang, surprising her from her thoughts. She picked up the portable handset and pushed the Call button without glancing at the caller ID. "Hello."

"Good morning, Charity. Guess who."

It took her a couple of heartbeats to recognize the voice. "Nathan?"

"Yeah, it's me. Been awhile. How are you?"

"I'm fine." She pushed her hair over her shoulder. "You?"

"I'm good. Real good. Where are you? The message on your mobile phone didn't say. Just gave this number to call."

"I'm at my folks' house in Kings Meadow for the summer. Cell service isn't reliable up here."

"Oh."

What do you want, Nathan?

As if she'd asked the question aloud, he said, "I was hoping to see you, Charity."

A confusion of feelings washed over her, completely mixed together so that she couldn't identify any of them singly.

"I could drive up there, if that's all right," he added after a lengthy silence.

"When?"

"Soon, I hoped. Today. Or tomorrow if that's better for you. Or next weekend."

A tiny, panicked feeling burst through the confusion. Did

she want to see Nathan? She had ended things between them because he wanted a different kind of life than she did.

"Charity?"

"I'm not sure it's a good idea, Nathan."

"Come on, Charity. Just to talk, to catch up. You've been on my mind a lot lately."

Would it change anything, seeing him? Then again, would it hurt anything? She supposed not. The end of their relationship hadn't been an ugly one. It had gone out on a whimper, not a roar.

"What do you say? A few hours. That's all I'm asking."

"All right. I suppose it would be okay. But I'm busy today. Come tomorrow afternoon, if you want. Say around two o'clock."

"Great. Thanks, Charity. I was only up there with you the one time, but I think I remember the way."

"Don't count on your memory. The streets around Kings Meadow can be confusing. Better print off a map." She gave him her parents' address and a few easy instructions as reminders.

"Great, Charity. I've got it. I'll see you tomorrow afternoon."

After pressing the End button, she put the handset back on the nightstand, still not sure how she felt about seeing Nathan again.

"Well, I guess I'll find out soon enough," she said to Cocoa.

The dog came over to the bed and waited for a pat on the head. Charity leaned down, looking Cocoa straight in the eyes. "You never liked Nathan the way you do Buck. Why is that?"

That train of thought would get her nowhere.

She rose and headed for the shower.

BUCK PUSHED OPEN THE GLASS DOOR AND STEPPED into a world of high-pitched giggles, ponytails, black leotards, and pink tights. Some girls sat on the floor, removing their dance shoes. Others were getting help from their mothers. Many of those same mothers noticed him and stopped what they were doing to stare—as if he were a creature from the dark lagoon. Instinct told him to turn around and leave this feminine domain. Immediately.

"Hi, Buck."

He turned to his left.

Skye Foster, the local dance teacher, smiled at him, laughter in her eyes. No doubt she knew a duck out of water when she saw one. "What can I do for you?" She walked toward him.

"Maybe I should come back. Looks busy in here."

"No." She shook her head. "I only have one class on Saturdays in the summer, and we just finished up. Everybody's getting ready to leave. Why don't you wait in my office?" She pointed toward an open door, amusement tugging at the corners of her mouth. "It's less chaotic in there than out here."

With a nod to Skye, he went into the small office. He couldn't blame her for laughing at him. He must have worn a strange expression. He liked kids and he'd always thought his two nieces hung the moon. But *that* many little girls in one place? Nerve wracking.

It didn't take long for the studio to empty out. When silence reigned again, he stepped into the office doorway. "Safe to come out?"

Skye laughed aloud this time. "It's safe. But the gossips will be wondering what a bachelor was doing at my Saturday ballet class."

"I did feel out of place." He chuckled. "I should have called you instead of coming over."

Her eyebrows arched in question.

"I got a harebrained idea this morning. I heard you give dance lessons to adults. Line dancing and swing and such. And I . . . I thought maybe I'd like to take a few lessons." He shrugged, then added, "It'll be good exercise for my ankle."

His ankle wasn't the real reason for his interest in lessons, but he wasn't about to admit it to Skye. The real reason was Charity. He'd watched her dance with other men on the night of the Fourth. He'd seen how much she enjoyed it. She was good at it too. His skills on the dance floor were okay but not great. That hadn't mattered in the past. It mattered now.

After yesterday's ride, he'd realized how much he would like to take Charity dancing. Take her out on a real date. He'd like to hold her in his arms and whirl her around a floor in time to the music. He'd like her to look up at him and smile, the way she'd done to other lucky guys three weeks ago. For Charity, he didn't want to be "good enough." He wanted to impress her. Because a woman like her didn't have to settle for "good enough." Not in anything.

Skye said, "I don't have another adult class starting until September. You could—"

"How about private lessons? Do you do those?" Man,

he sounded desperate. He didn't care for that. Then again, maybe he was desperate.

"Sometimes," she answered. "Is this for a special occasion? Like a wedding. I love to get a couple ready for that first dance as man and wife."

At the word *wedding*, Charity's image—this time in a cloud of white satin and lace—popped into Buck's head. He blinked it away. "Uh . . . no. No special occasion."

"Too bad." Something in her gaze said she didn't believe he was telling the whole truth.

Buck liked Skye Foster—in a kid-sister kind of way. Five years his junior, she was a petite and slender thing with straight black hair and dark-brown eyes. He'd always thought she resembled that actress Angie Harmon, in every way except height. A little bit of tomboy toughness. Not given to frills or froufrou. Always ready to laugh, but with a serious side as well.

"I could do an hour on Wednesday evenings at seven, if that would work for you," she said after a lengthy silence. "When would you like to start?"

"This coming Wednesday."

"This coming Wednesday it is. I'll see you at seven."

CLIPPITY DO-DA, THE BEAUTY SALON LOCATED around the corner from the library, was always a busy place on Saturdays. Midge Foster had opened her salon back in the late seventies, and almost every woman who lived in or around Kings Meadow eventually came through her door, either to see Midge or one of the two other stylists who worked for her.

Charity opened that door to Clippity Do-Da a few minutes before her scheduled appointment with Midge. A little bell announced her arrival. Conversations ebbed, all eyes turned in her direction, and then the chatter resumed.

"Have a seat, Charity," Midge called to her. "I'll be finished in a flash."

Charity went to one of the chairs by the large plate-glass window. After sitting, she grabbed one of the worn and torn beauty magazines and thumbed through it, not truly interested.

The bell rang again. Along with the others, Charity's gaze went to the door. This time the newcomer was Midge's daughter, Skye.

"Hi, hon," Midge said as she removed the cape from around her client's shoulders. "You done for the day?"

"Yeah. You'll never guess who—"

Midge held up a finger, silently asking for one minute. She went to the small counter, took her client's check, and booked the woman's next appointment. Then with swift efficiency, she swept up the hair on the floor around her chair and deposited it in a waste can.

"Come on over, Charity." Midge looked at her daughter again. "Sorry, hon. What were you about to tell me?"

Charity sat in the swivel salon chair, and Midge whipped a fresh cape around her.

Skye said, "Buck Malone came into the studio just as my class was letting out. He wants some private dance lessons."

"Well, good for him," Midge replied. "Wish more men would do that and save their sweethearts' toes."

"But Buck doesn't seem the type for lessons. Know what I mean? He gave some lame excuse that it would be good for strengthening his ankle." Skye lowered her voice. "I think what he really wants is to ask me out."

Charity felt a chill, as if the air conditioner was blowing right on her.

"Would you want him to ask you out?" Even as Midge asked Skye that question, her attention returned to Charity. "What do you want done?" she asked, their gazes meeting in the mirror. "Just a trim?" She raked her fingers through Charity's hair.

Charity nodded.

"How much off?"

She indicated about an inch with her thumb and index finger.

"Okay. Come over to the bowl and we'll give you a wash."

Skye followed them to the sink. "I don't know," she answered her mother as if there'd been no lull in the conversation. "I mean, he's awfully cute and all."

Midge laughed softly. "No argument from me. He can even make my old heart go pitty pat."

"*Mom!*" Skye drew out the word.

Whatever Midge said to her daughter next was lost behind running water and massaging fingers as Midge shampooed Charity's hair. Which was fine. She didn't need to listen in on that conversation. It had nothing to do with her. Nothing at all. She wasn't remotely interested.

Although it did surprise her about the lessons. Skye was right. Buck didn't seem the type to want them or even admit he needed them. Besides, most women wouldn't care if he knew fancy steps or not. They would just enjoy being held in his arms.

Skye would no doubt enjoy giving him those lessons too. She was his type. Rodeo queen and all that. Back in high school, he'd always gone out with girls like her. Why should it be different now? Perhaps it was more surprising that he, apparently, had never asked her out before now. If rumors were true, he'd dated most of the single gals in Kings Meadow already.

"Hey, Charity. Where'd you go?"

She opened her eyes.

"Thought you'd gone to sleep on me." Midge placed a towel over Charity's hair, easing her upright in the chair at the same time.

Skye gave her mom a little wave. "I'm meeting some friends for lunch. See you later." Her gaze flicked to Charity and she repeated the wave. Then she left the salon.

"Wish that girl would find the right guy," Midge said as Charity settled once again in the swivel chair before the large mirror. "She sure couldn't find a nicer one than Buck, so if he's interested, I'm all for it. Always have liked that young man, even when he seemed to be breaking every gal's heart between here and McCall."

Charity wished Midge would be quiet about Buck. It bothered her in a way she couldn't define.

"I was long married and had a couple of kids with a third in the oven by the time I was Skye's age."

Charity suddenly felt ancient.

"What is it with girls like you and Skye that you're still not married at your ages? Not that either of you are that old," Midge added quickly. "I know times are different now. We married younger in my day. And compared to my mother,

I was verging on being an old maid when I said 'I do.'" She leaned in a little closer, once again looking at Charity in the mirror. "So how's *your* love life, hon? Or are you too busy being a famous author to take time for romance?"

Heat rose in her cheeks.

"Don't you go all modest and humble on me with that blush. I've seen those write-ups in the newspaper and those national magazines. I keep hoping Hollywood will turn your books into a movie. They'd be so good up on the screen. Oh, they'd be so good." Midge began to trim Charity's hair with a small pair of scissors. "I used to think I'd like to write a novel. But there never seemed to be enough spare time, what with my business and raising a family. Now the nest's empty, and I'm just too blamed tired to try something new."

Charity gave Midge a smile, thankful that the woman's conversation had veered away from a discussion on her love life and toward the topic of writing. Still, she'd learned it was better to say nothing when others said they wanted to write a book. Unless they asked her point-blank for advice. Then she had a few simple but encouraging things to say.

Fortunately for Charity, Midge didn't ask any questions about writing a novel and seemed content to move on to other topics of interest to most residents of Kings Meadow.

Chapter 16

Upon his return from church that Sunday, Buck tied one of his horses in the shade of a large tree and began bathing the tall black gelding. His movements were slow, almost languid, befitting the heat of the day. Neither horse nor master minded being splashed by the cold water coming out of the hose.

Buck had finished rinsing the animal's coat when a small sports car—a convertible—pulled into his driveway. He straightened, then watched as the driver got out of the car. A frown wrinkled the stranger's brow and nose as he looked around. Eventually his gaze landed on Buck.

Buck wondered if the man could be someone wanting to book a trip into the wilderness, but he dismissed the notion at once. This was a city dude if ever he'd seen one. He wouldn't know the front end of a horse from the backside.

Buck turned the nozzle on the hose, shutting off the flow of water, and strode toward the man. "Can I help you?"

"Is this the Anderson house?"

"No. You came one place too far." He motioned with his head. "That's the Anderson home. But they aren't there at the moment."

"I'm here to see Charity. Not her parents."

Buck felt like grinding his teeth. Maybe it was the dismissive way the man had spoken. Or perhaps it was something about the way he almost smiled but didn't. Or maybe it was enough that he knew Charity.

"Sorry for troubling you," the fellow said.

Buck watched the stranger return to his car and waited until the convertible backed out of his driveway and pulled into the Andersons'. Then he returned to the gelding. He grabbed a brush and got back to business, glad he couldn't see the Andersons' front door from where he stood. Proud of himself for not even listening for the sound of Charity's voice when she answered the door. Still, he couldn't help wondering who the guy was and why he'd come to see her.

None of my business.

Maybe not, but he wanted it to be his business.

Who is he?

It didn't matter. Shouldn't matter. But still he wondered.

Maybe the guy was her contractor. Some contractors made a lot of money and drove fancy sports cars. Maybe he'd come to see her about the restoration of her house.

On a Sunday? Him come to see her? Not likely.

Again he felt like grinding his teeth.

He should have asked her out already. He should have gone over to her house the instant he admitted his feelings to himself. He didn't have to take her dancing on their first date. He could take her to dinner or a movie or both. He could impress her with his fancy footwork later on.

He put down the brush and moved away from the shade, not stopping until he could see the front of the Anderson home. He'd half hoped he would find the stranger still standing on the front steps, but he wasn't there. His convertible seemed to mock Buck from where it had been left in the driveway.

"You look great, Charity," Nathan said as she handed him a tall glass of iced tea.

"Thanks. You too." She settled onto the sofa opposite him.

Nathan's glance roamed the living room. "I was by your house this morning. Just happened to be in the neighborhood." His eyes returned to Charity. "What's going on there?"

"There was flood damage in May."

"Must have been right after we stopped seeing each other."

She continued as if he hadn't interrupted. "The insurance inspection revealed more problems than anticipated. So I've got a major renovation going on now. It'll last through the summer."

"Well, now I understand why you came up here to stay. I wondered. I always got the impression you didn't like being in Kings Meadow." He took a long drink from his glass before setting it on a coaster on a side table. "I turned into your neighbor's place by accident. He said your parents aren't here. Will they be home soon? It would be nice to see them again. I liked them a lot the time you brought me up here."

It was strange, the reluctance she felt to tell Nathan her parents wouldn't return until September. She couldn't think of a reason to feel that way. Yet she did. "No," she answered after a lengthy silence. "They won't be home soon. But when I see them, I'll tell them you were here and asked about them." Carefully chosen words that were completely true. Yet . . .

"Mmm." He looked at the glass of iced tea as if he might pick it up. "Charity, I'd like you to reconsider."

"Reconsider what?"

His gaze lifted to her again. "Us. You and me. We were good together. We were real good together."

"Nathan—"

"Hear me out. Please."

Reluctantly she nodded.

"Remember how you said you'd decided you'd like to get married and have kids? I just don't think you've thought that last part through. Not the baby part. I've seen the way you avoid ever being around them. You're like me. I'm not a baby kind of guy either."

Charity felt a sudden chill and crossed her arms over her chest, hugging herself.

"I'm sure about the kid thing, but maybe I was wrong to say I never want to get married. Maybe I'll change my mind about that eventually. But how will we know if you don't give us a chance?"

I don't want to wait to see if you'll change your mind. The thought surprised her. *I want a man who already knows what he wants.*

He leaned forward, forearms resting on his thighs. "Is there someone else?"

Buck's image flashed in her mind, but she shoved it away. That was a dead-end street. And besides, Buck was apparently interested in an adorable, dark-haired dance instructor.

"What do you say?" Nathan pressed. "Can we try again? See if we can rekindle some of that old spark."

"I'm up here for the rest of the summer." It wasn't exactly a refusal but not very encouraging either. "And with my deadline, I don't have time to be driving back and forth to Boise."

"You could come stay with me at my house until your place is done."

She drew back, surprised by his suggestion. She'd never let any relationship get to the place where living together had been a possibility. Besides, her newfound faith wouldn't allow it, and Nathan knew that. "I couldn't."

"I have an extra bedroom. You'd be a guest. What's wrong with that?"

"Nathan, it wouldn't look right to outsiders."

"We'd know we weren't doing anything wrong. Wouldn't be like we were sleeping together."

The past rushed at her. She knew only too well what could happen if she let her guard drop. Even sober, there was risk involved. Too much risk. Especially with the wrong guy.

Is Nathan the wrong guy?

He gave his head a slow shake. "All right. Bad suggestion. It's just that I want to see you. A lot. I want to make up for lost time." He stood and took a step toward her. "I want a chance, Charity. I've missed you, and I want us to try again."

Nerves quivering, she rose to her feet. Maybe she had made a mistake in ending things so abruptly. Maybe he'd deserved a chance to change his mind.

He took hold of her shoulders and kissed her, gentle and unhurried.

She waited. Waited to feel the old spark. Actually tried to feel it. It didn't happen. Not the way it used to. But perhaps all she needed was time.

Nathan kept hold of her shoulders when he drew his head back. "I could drive up on the weekends until your house is ready and you're home again."

"I have to write on Saturdays," she replied softly.

"Then Sundays. You can spare Sundays, can't you?"

At last she nodded. "I'm home from church a little after twelve o'clock."

"Good." He released her shoulders, grinning. "Now, what is there to do in this town on a Sunday afternoon?" Something in his tone implied *hick town* was what he meant.

She tamped down sudden irritation and answered, "Take a walk with the dog. Ride horses. Lie in the shade and read a book. Have a barbecue. Go fishing or whitewater rafting."

"Is there a movie theater?"

She shook her head. "No, but there's a store in town that still rents DVDs."

"No kidding?"

"No kidding."

"Decent restaurant?"

"Pretty decent."

He pressed his lips together, appearing to give his choices some thought. "Let's go fishing, then. I'm not much of a fisherman, but it'll give us time to catch up without any interruptions."

BUCK WAS BATHING THE FOURTH OF HIS SIX HORSES when Cocoa ambled over to say hi to him. He turned off the spray and leaned down to pet the dog.

"Cocoa," Charity called.

"Come on, girl." Buck left the shade and headed to the front yard. "She's here."

Standing in the driveway of the Anderson home, Charity looked in Buck's direction. She was dressed in shorts, sleeveless top, baseball cap, and sneakers and had a large canvas bag slung over her shoulder. The guy with the sports car stood not far behind her, fishing tackle in hand.

Once again, Buck felt that urge to grind his teeth.

"Come on, Cocoa," Charity called. "We're going fishing."

Cocoa shot away from Buck. He was no competition for an afternoon by the river.

Charity motioned for Buck to come over. When he neared the driveway, she said, "Buck, I'd like you to meet my . . . my friend, Nathan Gilbert."

Buck remembered the name from the night they'd shared the baked salmon dinner. Nathan had been her boyfriend for more than a year. She'd told Buck it hadn't worked out between them. So what was he doing in Kings Meadow, carrying fishing tackle?

Nathan stepped forward and held out his right hand. Fair-haired and handsome, he was a tall man, one who looked as if he spent regular hours every week lifting weights at a health club. There was an air of confidence and success about him too.

The two men shook hands. Buck was sorely tempted to start an arm-wrestling match, right there on the front lawn. He was certain he could take the guy down without a problem, despite Nathan's height and build.

Before the temptation could get the better of him, he loosened his grip, took a step back, and said, "Hope the fish are biting."

Something flickered across Charity's face. It was there and then gone, too fast for Buck to begin to figure out what she felt or thought. "See you later, Buck," she said before turning and walking toward her SUV.

"Have a good time," he called after her—but the twist in his gut told him he didn't mean it.

Chapter 17

THE BEST FISHING SPOT ON THE RIVER—A WELL-kept family secret—was located, as the crow flies, about six miles from the Anderson home. To reach it, one had to park a car or truck and then hike a fair stretch. Charity's dad had taken his two daughters there as far back as she could remember. She thought about going there with Nathan, but she couldn't do it. He wasn't family. She drove to a less secluded place with easy access from a parking spot adjoining the highway. Two other vehicles had arrived before them.

"Looks like we aren't the only ones who thought about fishing this afternoon," Nathan said as she opened her car door.

"It's not exactly a crowd. We'll find a bend in the river for ourselves." She opened the back door. "Come on, Cocoa." The dog hopped out.

Nathan carried the fishing gear. Charity carried a small cooler plus a canvas bag holding suntan lotion, bug spray, and a few other miscellaneous items. A well-worn path took them to the river, and as promised, Charity led the way to a place where no other fishermen were in sight.

"Been a long time since I did this," Nathan said as he set down the gear.

"My dad and I fish near my backyard just about every time he and Mom come down for a visit. He's caught some whoppers there. But this remains his favorite fishing grounds." She tugged on the brim of her baseball cap to block the glare of the sun. "I miss not getting to go fishing with him this summer."

"Why not? You'd think it would be easier than ever with you staying with them."

Darn. She hadn't wanted to tell him her folks were away.

"Charity?"

"Sorry. I forgot you didn't kn—" No, that wasn't true. She inhaled quickly and started again. "Mom and Dad are on vacation. In Europe."

"Wow. For how long?"

"The rest of the summer."

"Really?" His eyebrows rose. "So you're all by yourself up here?"

She shrugged. "Only as alone as I want to be. Remember. This is where I grew up. I know just about everybody in Kings Meadow." Deciding to change the subject, she reached for one of the fishing poles. "We're lucky it isn't as hot today as it has been. This'll be fun."

Charity's dad was an expert fly-fisherman, but fly-fishing felt like too much work to her. She preferred to cast the line and let the hook and lure sink beneath the surface of the water. She found it relaxing to slowly reel in the line while waiting—hoping—for a fish to strike. On the river, she didn't have to think or feel. She could simply enjoy the sounds of water in motion and of the breeze in the trees.

But being alone wasn't the purpose of this afternoon by the river. They were here so she could reconnect with Nathan after a few months apart. To see if she still had any feelings for him. So when her hook was baited, she didn't wander far afield as she normally would. Instead, she moved only far enough away that their lines wouldn't get tangled.

Sunlight glinted off the surface ripples. If not for her dark glasses, the brightness would have blinded her. She looked upriver, away from the sun, and cast the line into a deeper section of the water. A few moments later, Nathan tried to do the same. The attempt was slightly pathetic.

"Told you I haven't done much fishing."

She would have known that without him telling her.

After a lengthy silence, he said, "I never pictured you as a fishing kind of girl. You've always liked parties and crowds."

She shrugged. What could she say? That she'd been running from herself for more years than she cared to count. That she'd lost track of what mattered most to her without even realizing it. Those were truths that she'd only begun to grasp in the last year.

"Maybe it's the elevation." He jerked on his line, looking frustrated that nothing was there.

"What about the elevation?"

"Maybe you're different up here where the air is thinner."

She reeled in the line and cast a second time.

"Whatever it is, it looks good on you, Charity. But you always look good."

She waited for the compliment to cause a flutter of pleasure in her heart. But before that could happen, her pole arched.

"Hey, you've got something already!" Nathan shouted. He dropped his own pole on the bank and came to stand near her.

She reeled in the line, the way her dad had taught her to do, until the fish was out of the water.

"What is it?" Nathan asked.

She glanced over her shoulder to see if he was kidding. "A rainbow trout."

"Hmm. Looks big. Is it? For a trout, I mean."

"It's a nice one." She heard impatience in her voice and tried to cover it when she said, "Bet you'll catch the next one."

"That's all right. It's more fun to watch you."

Charity baited her hook, then waded into the river, the water only mid-calf deep where she stood. It was a few moments before she realized she'd walked into the water to get farther away from Nathan. Not a positive sign.

Hot and sweaty, Buck stood at the kitchen sink and guzzled a third glass of water. He was tired, but it was a good kind of tired. He'd accomplished a lot this afternoon. But it was time for him to get his right leg elevated. He hadn't been on his feet for this long of a stretch since before Cocoa knocked him flat, and the ache in his ankle told him he was going to regret it. His wrist had a few complaints of its own.

His stomach growled, reminding him it had been a long

time since lunch. But he wanted to clean up more than he wanted food. He set the empty glass next to the sink and headed for the bathroom. It didn't take him long to shed his dirty clothes, shower, and get dressed again in clean Levis and a black T-shirt. Barefooted, he was on his way back to the kitchen when he heard Cocoa's bark. The sound drew him to the living room window.

Charity's Lexus was back in the Anderson driveway, parked not too far from the convertible. Charity stood near the back of her vehicle while Nathan carried fishing poles and a tackle box into the garage. While she watched Nathan, Buck watched her. Did she look wistful? Sorry the day at the river was over? Happy to have been with that guy? What?

Buck's telephone rang. A welcome interruption. He went to answer it. "Hello?"

"Hi, Buck. It's Chet."

"Hey, Chet."

"We've had a last-minute trail ride request from some guests for tomorrow morning. You up for it?"

"Sure. I'm up for it."

"It's a good-sized group. Two families. Four adults and five kids. Youngest of the kids is ten. The rest are teens. They'd like about a four-hour ride, round trip. I figured the best trail would take them up near McHenry's Sluice and down again."

At the mention of McHenry, Buck's thoughts tried to wander to Charity again. He brought them back into focus. "Any riding experience among them?"

"Some, apparently, but not much. I'd go with you, but I've got an appointment I can't put off."

"No need. I've taken larger groups on harder trails all by myself."

They went over a few details, including what time Buck should arrive at the ranch the next morning, horse trailer in tow. He was dropping the handset into its cradle when a knock sounded on his back door. When he looked through the window, he saw a baseball cap and blond ponytail.

He grinned. He didn't know what had brought Charity over, but he was glad she'd come. As long as that Nathan guy wasn't still with her. That thought wiped the smile from his mouth as he went to open the door. But it returned quickly enough when he found her alone, except for her dog and a string of rainbow trout.

"Have you had dinner?" she asked.

"Nope."

"Would you like to share my catch?"

"Sure." He opened the door wider. "Nathan joining us?" The words almost choked him on the way out of his mouth.

"No. He had to get back to Boise. Some big meeting he has to prepare for tomorrow."

"Come on in." Buck took a step back and motioned for her to come through.

"Oh, I didn't bring the fish so we could eat at your place. I just wanted to tempt you with what's for dinner."

He shrugged. "I don't mind if you use my kitchen. You're more familiar with it than I am by now."

"No. Please. Come over to the house in forty-five minutes."

"Can I bring anything?"

"No." She shook her head. "See you soon." She turned away and hurried toward her parents' home.

Buck forgot to be tired, achy, or even hungry. All he knew was he was having dinner with Charity.

And Nathan Gilbert wasn't.

CHARITY TOOK THE FASTEST SHOWER ON RECORD and was in the kitchen well before Buck was due to arrive. She cut up red potatoes, baby carrots, scallions, and turnips. By the time the vegetables were sautéed and put into the oven to roast and caramelize, the forty-five minutes she'd asked for were gone. Buck knocked on the back door right on time.

"Come in," she called as she laid one of the fish in the hot skillet, then a second beside the first. From the corner of her eye, she saw Buck stop in the kitchen doorway. "Dinner will be ready in about ten more minutes."

"Want me to set the table?"

"Sure." She directed him with her eyes. "The plates are in that cupboard there. Silverware in that drawer."

They didn't try to talk above the loud sizzling coming from the stove, and that was fine with Charity. She needed to concentrate on the fish. She wanted them to be perfect when they came out of the pan. Silly that it mattered so much to her. She'd cooked for Buck before. The only thing different this time was the location. Her mom's kitchen instead of Buck's.

It wasn't long before they were seated across from each other at the dining room table. Charity bowed her head as Buck prayed over the meal, and she couldn't help noticing how good it felt, listening to him talk to God. After he said, "Amen," she handed him the platter of fish, followed by the bowl of vegetables.

When Buck took his first bite, he made a sound of appreciation and grinned at her. "Your mom would be proud."

Charity felt a blush rise in her cheeks.

He changed the subject. Perhaps he took pity on her. "I'm taking some Ultimate Adventures guests on a trail ride tomorrow."

"You'll be back to work so soon?"

He nodded. "It'll be a repeat of the ride you and I did on Friday. Hey, you wouldn't care to join us, would you?"

She almost said yes. She wanted to. Really wanted to. "Sorry. I can't." Before she could stop herself, she added, "Perhaps some other time."

"Okay. I'll hold you to that." The warm look in his eyes promised he meant it.

It was nice to have Buck Malone for a friend. He'd said that's what they were. And a girl couldn't have too many friends. Right?

Chapter 18

ALEC CONNORS SHOOK BUCK'S HAND. "THANKS FOR a great day. I'm a history lover, so I've got to say this ride topped even the whitewater rafting. Will I be able to find books about the gold rush and McHenry in the bookstore I saw in town?"

"I'm sure Heather—she's the owner of Heather Books— has a good selection on the history of these mountains and the Boise Basin gold rush," Buck answered. "Zeb McHenry gets a mention in some of the history books, but I don't think anybody's ever written a whole book about him."

"You ought to do it. You're a natural storyteller."

Buck laughed. "I've got a neighbor who's a writer, but I doubt I'll ever be one. I like horses more than words." He patted the side of the horse trailer for emphasis. "If you go to the bookstore, tell Heather I sent you."

"I will. In fact, I think I'll drive into Kings Meadow today and check it out."

Other members of the party came over to thank Buck for the trip before walking away from the trailers.

"Well," Chet said when it was just the two of them, "you were a hit."

Buck turned to face him. "More like the horses and scenery were a hit. Didn't hurt that Mr. Connors is a school teacher and loved learning something new."

Chet opened the back of one of the trailers and unloaded the first horse. "Hope you like telling your stories, because I'm sure you and the trail rides are going to get rave reviews on the Web site. All of the guests will be wanting the same experience from here on out."

"Wouldn't mind it." Buck led a second horse away from the trailer. "Enjoyed myself, more than I thought I would."

Chet's youngest son, Pete, showed up to help, and it didn't take long for the three of them to unload the remainder of the Leonard stock from the two trailers. When only Buck's gelding remained, he closed the back of his four-horse trailer and got into his truck.

Chet came to the door of the cab. "We've got more guests arriving tomorrow. I'll give you a call as soon as I know when we'll need you next."

"Okay."

Buck turned the key in the ignition as Chet took a step back. With a wave, Buck pulled on out. He left the windows down, the hot summer air blowing in as the truck rolled along the two-lane highway toward home. It felt good to be working again. And if Chet's ideas panned out, the work would keep Buck busy almost full-time.

"Thanks, Lord," he said softly.

His thoughts veered to Charity. Not a surprise. He'd thought of her often during the ride today. As he'd pointed things out to the guests or shared a bit of history, he'd pictured Charity on the day of their ride to the same location, along that same trail. He'd heard her voice, pictured her smile. He'd remembered her reaction to the Riverton estate, and he'd felt again the desire to take care of her, to shelter her, to be there for her when she needed him.

He wanted her to need him.

Am I falling in love with her?

He tested the words in his heart, rolled them around in his mind.

Have I already fallen?

He couldn't be sure. He'd never been in love with a woman before. For years he'd been too busy caring for his dad and then his mom, working overtime, working more than one job. Later, when it was just himself to look out for, he hadn't wanted a serious relationship. He'd never let himself consider something more.

Now he was considering it.

It wasn't in Buck's nature to quit without giving his all. He owed it to himself—maybe he owed it to Charity too—to see where his feelings might lead.

"I have to find out," he whispered, the words whisked away by the wind.

CHARITY PUT DOWN THE PEN AND CLOSED THE JOURnal. Then she reached for a tissue and wiped her eyes.

Soul searching was an exhausting endeavor. Self-analysis

ROBIN LEE HATCHER

seemed never ending. She'd done so much of it over the past year. But the events and emotions of recent weeks had finally convinced her that she needed to dig ever deeper. That's what she'd tried to do today. She'd tried to bare her soul in the pages of the journal.

It had surprised her when she began writing about the day she'd realized she was pregnant. It was shocking to see those words upon the page, black ink on off-white paper, detailing the emotions that had overtaken her on that cold February afternoon. The same emotions overwhelmed her now.

There was a quote she'd seen on the Internet that said, "You're only as sick as your secrets." If that was true, Charity was sicker than she wanted to be, sicker than she was willing to remain. And that was a step in the right direction.

After sitting a moment, thinking it through, she reached for the telephone. She needed to make a call now before she lost her nerve. Drawing a deep breath, she punched in her sister's number.

Terri answered before the second ring. "Hey, Charity."

"Hi, Terri."

"I'm glad you called. We haven't talked since we were there for the weekend."

"I know. I've been writing a lot."

Terri sighed. "Aren't you ever going to listen to me? You need to get out more often. It isn't good for you to shut yourself up the way you do."

"I have to shut myself away. I've got a deadline."

"But you aren't dead yet."

This wasn't going the direction Charity had planned. "Terri, I need a favor."

170

"What's that?"

"I called because I need to tell you something. I need you to listen until I'm all done talking. No comments. No gasps. Nothing but silence. Do you think you can do that for me?"

There was a long pause, then, "I'll promise to do my best."

"Thank you." *But how do I begin?* She searched for the right words. "Something happened to me when I was at BSU. In the winter, just before I turned twenty. I know that seems a long time ago, but sometimes, to me, it's like it's happened again and again."

She drew a quick breath and continued. The words came slowly at first. She stumbled a few times and had to go back and fill in the gaps. But the more she talked, the faster the words came until they were pouring out of her, like water over a spillway.

Until now, no one but Charity and Jon Riverton had known what happened that night in his bedroom in the mansion. Only she had known how her alcohol haze had made the room spin, how she'd had no strength to resist his forceful seduction. She'd been a naïve, inexperienced virgin, unprepared for what was about to happen, too gullible for words, too eager to please. She told her sister everything—her failure to scream, to refuse, the copious tears she'd wept when it was over, how violated she'd felt, the guilt that took hold, the callous way Jon had put her in a chauffeured automobile and had her driven back to Boise. Already discarded.

And then she told Terri about the pregnancy, about Jon's threats—frightening and detailed—of what he would do if she told anyone. Particularly if she told his father. The pressure he'd exerted to force her to have an abortion. The hatred she'd felt—for him, for herself, even for the baby inside of her—as she counted down the months, waiting for the ordeal to be over. She admitted it all—her deepest, darkest sins, her unending shame.

She held nothing back.

Her sister never made a sound.

At last, Charity's words dried up. She closed her eyes and waited for a response.

"Oh, Pipsqueak." Terri's voice broke over a sob.

Charity had made it through the confession without breaking down, but once she knew her sister wept, her own tears began to flow.

"Finally," Terri said, "it begins to make sense. Why you didn't like to come home. You didn't want to run into him. You didn't want to be reminded."

A lump formed in Charity's throat.

"What I wouldn't do if I could get my hands on him. I'm glad his life caught up with him. I hope he's miserable, wherever he is now."

She almost smiled at the big-sister response.

Terri was silent for a few moments. Then, in a more determined tone than before, she said, "I'm not going to give you a sermon or a pep talk, sis. But I think you need to do a couple of things. First, you need to find a counselor."

"I've tried counseling. More than once."

"Try again. Get a good counselor who can walk you through the healing process. You've been punishing yourself long enough."

Punishing myself. Was that what she'd been doing all this time? Punishing herself?

"And . . . you're going to have to tell Mom and Dad what you just told me."

"I don't know if I can," Charity whispered.

"You can. You've taken the first step. It'll get easier."

Charity dried her eyes with another tissue. "You always sound so sure of yourself."

"Helps that I'm always right."

"Uh-huh." This time she did smile, though briefly.

"Sis, I'm proud of you for telling me. It took courage."

"I don't feel very courageous," she replied.

"Listen, maybe I am going to give a sermon. Charity, you did a really dumb thing when you were nineteen. You got drunk and you went somewhere you shouldn't have gone with a boy who flattered you and then betrayed you. You got pregnant, but even though you were scared and unhappy, you didn't abort the baby. You made plans to give it up for adoption. You took a bad situation and tried to do the right thing. But then you lost your child. That's a pain no woman forgets. You've got emotional scars. That's obvious. And you've let fear sabotage your relationships with men and with your family for way too long. But you've done a lot of stuff to be proud of too. You got your degree, even though you could have dropped out of school. You've written three books and started a new career and supported yourself the whole time. And recently you've seen where you weren't living right and you made decisions to change those things. That's courage, Charity, and you've got a lot of it inside of you."

Wow, she mouthed, but no sound came out.

Terri released a short, mirthless laugh. "Sorry. I couldn't hold it back any longer."

Charity cleared her throat. "I think I'm glad you didn't."

"I love you, sis."

"I love you too."

"Let's talk again in a day or two."

"Okay."

After they said good-bye, Charity went into the living room and lay on the sofa, hugging a throw pillow to her chest. She felt drained. Empty, but in a good way. Her sister's "sermon" replayed in her head, and an unfamiliar peace seemed to fall over her, like a down comforter.

Before long, exhausted, she slept.

Chapter 19

Smiling, Skye Foster released Buck's hand and went to pause the CD player before the next song began. When she turned around again, she said, "You're a natural, Buck. You'll be ready to turn pro in a few weeks."

He grinned back at her. "No, thanks. All I want to do is impress a girl."

"Who?" she asked, the smile fading.

"Not sure I want to say yet."

She stared at him, obviously planning to stay silent and stand still until he answered her question.

"All right. If you must know, Charity Anderson."

Skye's eyes widened a little. Then she smiled again. "Charity. Really? And here I thought you were taking dance lessons so you could spend time with me."

"You did? I mean, I—"

"Stop, Buck." She held up a hand like a traffic cop. "Stop before you say something that'll embarrass us both. I was teasing." She mumbled something that sounded like *mostly* as she turned back to the CD player. "Let's do one more. Then we'll call it a night."

It was a slow song. No fast footwork required.

As they began to turn around the floor, Skye looked up at him. "Weren't you and Charity in the same class in school?"

"Yeah, but I didn't know her very well."

"Haven't you taken out all of the single girls you knew back then?"

He gave his shoulders a slight shrug.

Skye persisted. "But you never dated Charity, huh?"

"No, we never dated."

"Not your type?" Skye intruded on his thoughts with another question. "What makes her your type now? Why do you like her?"

Buck thought of how pretty Charity was. He thought of her warmth, her sense of humor. She was smart and engaging. She was sophisticated, yet down to earth. She loved dogs and horses. They shared a similar upbringing. They shared the same faith, although Charity was less vocal about hers.

He'd known lots of women who'd shared many similar qualities, but they still hadn't changed his mind about commitment, about settling down, about giving away his heart. What made Charity different?

"None of my business," Skye said, a wry smile curving one corner of her mouth. "But from the look on your face, I'd say you've got it bad for her. Must be love."

The comment jolted him, brought him to a stop on the dance floor.

Skye took a step back. "Sorry. I shouldn't have said that. *Really* none of my business."

"No." He shook his head. "It's okay. But maybe it's time to call it a night, like you said."

"Okay. Next Wednesday. Same time."

"I'll be here." Buck went for the hat that he'd left on a chair and set it on his head. By the time he turned around, Skye had shut off the music, plunging the dance studio into silence. "Thanks. I appreciate your help."

"You're welcome, Buck. It's my pleasure. Really." She brushed her long black hair over her shoulder. "And good luck with Charity."

"Thanks."

He left the studio, pausing outside to look down the street. Kings Meadow pretty much rolled up the sidewalks in the evenings. By this time on a week night, most diners had departed the restaurant on the western edge of town, but the bar half a block off Main was beginning to gain customers. From the opposite direction, he heard some shouting. Young male voices. An evening game of touch football in the park, most likely. Rather than go to his truck, he turned toward the sounds and began walking. The heat of the day had mellowed and shadows had grown long.

Buck had guessed right. A game of touch football was in progress. High school kids from the look of them. Even a couple of girls were in the game, while a few more stood off the playing field, shouting encouragement to their boyfriends.

Buck bumped the brim of his hat with his knuckles as he crossed the street to observe from the sidelines. He recognized quite a few of them, knew some of their parents from church or businesses around town. Of course Ken would know them all. He was that kind of high school principal. His brother knew every kid and every parent. Even knew most home situations—what families were struggling financially, what couples were on the brink of divorce, what kid was in danger of sliding out of the educational system altogether.

As boys, on many a summer's evening, Buck and Ken had joined friends for games of touch football or baseball, either here in the park or over at the old high school field. There'd always been girls on the sidelines then, like now. Sara shouting for Ken and one girl or another cheering on Buck.

"I'd say you've got it bad for her. Must be love."

As Skye's words drifted in his memory, he imagined himself in the game and Charity on the sidelines, rooting for him. It surprised him, how much he'd like to make that come true.

CHARITY HAD DEVELOPED A CRICK IN HER NECK BY the time she stopped writing. In the living room, a rerun of a cop show played on the television. She glanced at the wall clock. It was half past eight. She rolled her head from side to side, then forward and back, trying to ease the stiffness.

"I'm hungry," she said aloud. "Cocoa? Are you hungry?"

She waited for her dog to come into the kitchen. Then she remembered she'd let Cocoa into the backyard before sitting down to write again after watching the news.

"Sorry, girl." Charity rose and walked through the kitchen to the back door. "Cocoa! Come," she called. But her dog didn't come running as usual. She pushed open the screen door and stepped outside. "Cocoa!" No response.

A flutter of alarm filled her chest as she went down the steps. She hurried to the side of the house to make sure Cocoa wasn't sleeping under the blue spruce. Not there either. The side gate wasn't open, nor was the back gate. Where on earth was she?

"Cocoa, come!"

As she headed once again to the back door, she heard the sound of Buck's truck a few moments before it pulled into view. He parked it next to the horse trailer and cut the engine.

"Buck!" She left the yard and trotted toward the truck.

He took one look at her face and the smile on his own faded. "What's wrong?" He hopped down from the cab.

"It's Cocoa. I can't find her. She got out of the yard somehow. I let her outside two hours ago, but I only just discovered she was gone. Buck, she never goes far from home. Never. And she always comes when I call. You know how obedient she is."

"Yeah. I know. Don't worry. We'll find her." He turned toward the east. "That's the way you usually go on your walks, isn't it?"

She nodded, though he wasn't looking at her.

"Let's try that way first. Come on." He glanced over his shoulder. "Like you said, she wouldn't go far, and this road doesn't get much traffic. We'll find her."

She wanted to believe him. Needed to believe him. It had only been a couple of days since she'd poured out her heart to Terri. Two days of feeling as if she'd turned a corner. But if something had happened to Cocoa . . .

God, please let her be okay. Please.

They set off down the road, falling into a rhythm of

calling Cocoa's name, first one, then the other. Otherwise, neither of them spoke. They stared at the fields and pastures, looking for some sign of the dog. With each passing minute, Charity grew a little more afraid that something bad had happened to her faithful friend. Tears welled in her eyes and she had to blink them back. Another hour or so and it would grow dark. What if they didn't find her before sunset?

Although Charity didn't make a sound, somehow Buck must have known when she began to cry. He stopped, took hold of her, and drew her into his embrace. That was a mistake, for it gave her permission to let the dam burst. She pressed her face into his shirt and sobbed.

Buck gently rubbed her back with the flat of his hand and murmured words of comfort that she couldn't quite make out. It didn't matter. She was comforted by them anyway. She wished she could stay within the circle of his arms forever.

But she couldn't. Drawing a shaky breath, she pulled away from him. "Sorry," she whispered. "I know she's only a dog."

"No such thing as '*only* a dog.' And we're going to find her. Don't give up hope."

She swiped the tears from her cheeks with her fingertips. "I won't. I'm not."

He gave her a sympathetic smile.

"She's never run away before." She sniffed. "I don't know what I'd do without her."

"You won't have to. We'll find her. Come on. Let's keep going while we've got daylight."

But they didn't find Cocoa, and eventually they had to turn back. Charity felt as if her heart was breaking. If she hadn't become so involved in her writing, leaving Cocoa outside for so long, the dog wouldn't be lost now. She was sure of it. This was her fault. Her fault. Her fault.

Darkness shrouded them by the time they got back. Buck's house was completely dark. The flicker of the television was the only light coming from the Anderson home.

Buck said, "We'll start looking again at dawn."

Charity nodded, her chest heavy. She wished Buck would take her in his arms again. She wished he would hold her for a long, long time.

"Try to get some sleep," he added.

She knew she wouldn't sleep a wink.

"Wish there was more I could do."

"I know," she whispered. Then, "Thanks, Buck."

"See you in the morning."

"In the morning."

She turned and moved away from him. When she reached the back stoop, she sank onto it and hid her face in her hands. She didn't weep as she had earlier. She felt too broken for tears.

BUCK HAD BEEN IN BED, THE LIGHTS OUT, FOR A good half hour or more when he felt the strongest need to search his pasture for Charity's dog. To search it *now*. It seemed a crazy idea. If she'd been that close to home, Cocoa would have heard her mistress calling. But the feeling wouldn't go away and so he obeyed, tossing aside the sheet. It didn't take long to pull on jeans, T-shirt, and boots. Then he headed for the back door.

The night air was cool, and the moon had risen, casting a soft white glow over the valley. But Buck didn't need moonlight or the flashlight he carried to know his way to the pasture gate. Two of his horses were nearby. One nickered to him, as if asking what he was doing out there at this hour.

"Cocoa," he called softly as he closed the gate behind him.

He decided to follow the fence around the perimeter of the pasture. If he didn't find the dog there—did he even expect to find her?—he would try crisscrossing the acreage.

He started off, counterclockwise, calling her name in the same soft tone. Not loud enough to wake his neighbor if her window was open, but loud enough for a dog's ears. He swept the beam of the flashlight back and forth in a wide arc, both inside the fence and beyond it. Nothing. No sign of her. But he kept going.

On the backside of his property, across the creek and beyond the trees, he stopped still. The sound of water splashing over rocks was all he heard.

"Cocoa."

No. He was wrong. There was another sound. A whimper.

Buck whipped the flashlight to the north, beyond the fence. "Cocoa."

Another whimper. Almost too soft to hear but definitely there.

He slipped through the fence onto the neighboring land. It took him another five minutes to find the dog, partially hidden by a bush in the corner of the fences. As he pushed the greenery aside, the flashlight revealed a nasty gash on her back. The odd angle of her front leg told him it was broken.

"What happened to you, girl?" he said, although he suspected Cocoa had tangled with a bear from the look of the injuries.

He debated what he should do. Leave her there and call the vet. Or pick her up and carry her home. Both had downsides, but he thought leaving her had the most risk. He pulled off his T-shirt and ripped it up one side. Using it as a bandage, he wrapped the shirt around Cocoa to protect the wound on her back. He couldn't do much about her leg except try to stabilize it with a stick and another piece of fabric.

"All right, Cocoa. I'll try not to hurt you more."

The dog whimpered in pain as he lifted her, even jerked her head as if she wanted to snap at him but didn't have the strength.

"It's okay, Cocoa. It's okay."

The hardest part was getting her through the fence. After that, Buck moved at a fast walk toward the house. As he slipped through the gate, he had another decision to make. Go into his house and call the vet or awaken Charity and call the vet from her place. No, there really wasn't a choice. He had to take Cocoa to her mistress now.

In the moonlight, he saw that the window of a second-story bedroom was open to the night air. Had to be Charity's room since no one else was home. He stopped beneath it and called out, "Charity. I found Cocoa. Let me in."

It took only a few moments for her head to appear in the opening.

"She's hurt, Charity. Let me in. We need to call the vet."

Without a word, she was gone, no doubt running for the stairs. By the time Buck had climbed the few steps on the back stoop, the door had opened before him.

When Charity saw the now-bloody T-shirt wrapped around Cocoa, she covered her mouth with one hand, as if trying to hold back her shock. But a moment later, she removed her hand, saying, "Put her on the table. What's the name of the vet?"

"I'll call him." Buck placed the dog on the kitchen table. "You stay with Cocoa. She'll be easier with you near." He went to the phone, picked up the handset, and punched in the number. He knew it by heart.

The vet answered on the third ring. "Hello?"

"Devon. It's Buck Malone. We've got an injured dog here at the Anderson place. Looks to me like she got into a scrape with a bear. She's got a deep gash on her back and a broken leg. Shall I bring her to the clinic?"

"No. I'll come to you. I just finished an emergency call and was about to head home. Give me ten minutes." The vet hung up without saying good-bye.

Buck turned around. "He's on his way."

Leaning over Cocoa while stroking the dog's head, Charity glanced up. "A bear?"

"Most likely."

"Where did you find her?"

"Beyond my back fence. The McClellan property."

She rubbed Cocoa's ear between two fingers as she straightened. "How did you happen to look there?"

"Just a hunch." He shrugged. "A feeling I couldn't ignore."

Thank you, she mouthed before her gaze returned to the dog on the table. "Hold on, Cocoa. The vet will be here soon."

IT WAS LONG AFTER MIDNIGHT BY THE TIME DR. Devon Parry drove away from the Anderson home, his sedated patient's back stitched and bandaged, her leg secured with a splint. When Charity could no longer see the lights of the vet's truck, she turned back into the house. Buck was in the kitchen, rubbing disinfectant spray that the vet had left across the table surface. He stopped when he saw her.

"Better not tell your mother that her kitchen became an operating room for a dog." He gave her a teasing smile.

Surprisingly, she laughed, even as tears welled in her eyes. "Agreed. It'll be our secret."

Tenderness filled his expression. "Cocoa's going to be all right."

"Thanks to you." She swallowed the hot lump in her throat.

He resumed wiping.

"You don't have to do that. It's late. You should go home and get some sleep. You've done so much already."

Her hand covered the back of his and he stopped still.

When had she leaned across the table? How had her lips moved so close to his?

A muscle jerked in his jaw. His gaze seemed hot upon her skin. She drew back slightly, then was pulled by some invisible means toward him again.

Their lips met. Only their lips. Softly. Sweetly.

The room seemed to hold its breath right along with the two people in it.

Yes, she held her breath. Held it for a long time. Too long. What else could explain the dizziness that swept over her? The weakness in her knees. The inability to string a rational thought together. When Buck drew back, Charity sucked in air, all the while wishing he would make her hold her breath again with another kiss.

No. No, she shouldn't want him to kiss her again. Didn't want him to. His friendship had become important to her. She didn't want to lose it. And she would lose it if she allowed him to think they could enjoy a brief summer fling. She straightened—and almost fell over a chair. Instead, she dropped onto it.

"Hey," Buck said, "are you all right?" He rounded the table, looking concerned.

"I'm fine. I'm fine." She lifted a hand to ward him off. "It's just . . . It's been a difficult night. I'm tired. I think you'd better go."

His eyes narrowed. A crease appeared between his brows. "Sure. Of course." He took a step back. "You'll let me know how Cocoa's doing?"

She nodded.

"Good night, Charity."

"Good night," she whispered, lowering her gaze to her hands, folded in her lap.

A few moments later, she heard the closing of the back door. Silence surrounded her. So silent she could hear her own breathing. The emptiness was almost too painful to bear. She needed Cocoa.

But she wanted Buck.

BUCK STOOD IN HIS BACKYARD, STARING AT THE Anderson home. He saw when the kitchen light went off. He saw the light go on in the second-floor bedroom, then moments later go out again.

I shouldn't have kissed her. The timing was all wrong.

He would blame it on how adorable she'd looked in her blue-and-white print pajama bottoms and oversized T-shirt with the image of a kitten stamped on the front. Her long hair had fallen free over her shoulders and down her back, delightfully disheveled. And with the crisis over, with her hand on top of his, it had been the most natural thing in the world to lean close and kiss her.

He'd thought she wanted it too. There was no doubt that she'd kissed him back. No doubt. And she hadn't pushed him away. So why, all of a sudden, had her defenses gone up?

"You confuse me, Charity Anderson."

He swiveled on his heel and went into the house. But he didn't return to the bedroom. It would be pointless to try to sleep now. Instead, he started a pot of decaf brewing, grabbed his Bible off the bookshelf in the living room, and sat down at the kitchen table. Maybe he could glean a nugget or two of wisdom from between its covers. His instincts obviously weren't enough in this situation.

"I like her, God. I like her a lot. Maybe I'm even falling in love with her. I never wanted that to happen, but maybe You do."

Willie Nelson's voice snuck into his head, singing, *"To all the girls I've loved before."*

He sighed. "Lots of girls, lots of women, but nobody I've loved. I thought that was all I wanted. I thought it would keep my heart safe. I'm not so sure anymore."

With another sigh, he opened the battered leather cover of his Bible, flipping through the pages until he arrived at 1 Corinthians 13. The famous love chapter. Had he ever attended a wedding where at least a few of those verses weren't used during the ceremony? Not one he remembered, anyway.

He began to read, slowly, with purpose, meditating on a verse or two at a time, going back, reading them again. He measured himself against the highest ideal represented in the chapter and mentally winced. Patient and kind. Never jealous or arrogant. Not wanting his own way and never taking into account a wrong suffered. Added all together, that was a tall order.

But he thought it would be worth trying with Charity. Now all he had to do was make her want to do the same with him.

Chapter 20

THE KINGS MEADOW ANIMAL CLINIC WAS LOCATED south of town on Old Fitzgibbon Road. Owned by Devon Parry, the veterinary clinic was equipped for the care of both small and large animals, although much of the vet's large-animal work was still conducted by visits to the ranches and farms he served.

Charity arrived at nine o'clock at the vet clinic, just as the receptionist was unlocking the front door. Devon himself led her to a back room where cages lined two walls. Most of them were empty, and Charity spied Cocoa almost at once. The dog lifted her head and whimpered as Charity approached.

"Hello, girl," she said softly.

Cocoa's right leg was in a cast. A large portion of her back and side had been shaved in Charity's mom's kitchen, revealing pink flesh and a row of neat stitches that closed the wound.

She squatted beside the cage. "May I open the door?"

"As long as she doesn't get too excited. We want her to stay quiet."

"She'll stay if I tell her to." Charity reached for the latch. "Cocoa, stay." She lifted the handle and slid the latch to the side. Cocoa slapped her tail on the floor of her cage three times in slow succession. Charity stroked the dog's head. "How long will she need to stay?"

"I'd like to keep an eye on her for a couple of days. Just to make sure the wound doesn't get infected. Don't worry. We'll take good care of her."

"I know." She stared into Cocoa's eyes, willing the dog to understand why she had to stay in a cage in this bright, white, ultra-clean room. "So I should be able to come get her Saturday?"

"Yes, as long as she doesn't start running a fever."

Charity drew in a long breath and gave Cocoa a few more strokes as a farewell. After latching the cage door, she stood. Cocoa sighed and closed her eyes.

"She's a lucky dog," the vet said. "Could have ended much worse than this."

"I don't understand how she got out of the yard, let alone why she tangled with a bear."

"Maybe Cocoa thought you were in danger. A bear sniffing around close by is probably all it would take. From what Buck said, she's protective of you. Isn't that what caused his fall when he broke his ankle? Wasn't Cocoa trying to protect you?"

"Yes, I guess so."

In unison, they turned toward the front office and started walking.

Devon said, "I let the sheriff know there was a bear attack on a dog and that folks should be on the lookout."

At the exit, Charity bid the vet a good day and then went to her car. She didn't feel like going home to the empty house. When she'd arrived in Kings Meadow in early June, she'd made a point of discouraging any and all visitors from dropping by, claiming the need for privacy while she worked. It hadn't taken a great deal of effort on her part for that word to get around, and folks had honored her request for solitude. But now she wished for company.

However, the person she wanted to see most was the same person she most wanted to avoid: Buck.

So instead she went to see Sara again. Perhaps, in part, she wanted more than the company of a good friend. Perhaps it was a sort of test. Would her confession to Terri make seeing the baby easier this time? Had all of her soul-searching changed her for the better, perhaps made her stronger?

It didn't take long to drive to Sara's. A couple of cars were in the driveway, so she parked at the curb. It was the oldest girl, Krista, who answered the door.

"Hi. Is your mom—" Charity began.

"She's in the kitchen." Leaving the door open, the girl hurried toward the family room, the sounds of a video game, and teenage laughter.

Smiling to herself, Charity said, "Thanks," although she doubted she was heard. Then she followed the hall to the kitchen.

Sara, seated at the table near a bay window, saw Charity just before she stepped into the room. "Hi, Charity."

Charity was about to reply when another step brought

Ashley Holloway into view. Before her on the table was an open three-ring binder, filled with pages and multicolored dividers.

"Get yourself a cup of coffee and come join us," Sara said.

Ashley added, "Sara's helping me with final details for the reunion. We'd love your input too."

A little disappointed that she wouldn't have Sara all to herself, Charity went to the coffeepot, took a mug from a wooden mug tree nearby, and reached for the carafe. After filling the mug with coffee and adding some creamer, she carried it to the table and sat in the chair across the table from Ashley and Sara.

"That looks like a ton of work," she said, her gaze on the binder.

"We're expecting over two hundred people to come to the reunion," Ashley answered with a smile. It changed to a frown as she added, "But *you* haven't signed up yet."

Charity shrugged. "I've been so busy I keep forgetting."

"Well, let's take care of that right now." Ashley flipped through the binder to a page with a color photo of Charity at seventeen.

"Oh my word," she whispered. Did school photos get much worse than that one?

Ashley didn't seem to hear. "We've got golfing on Saturday up in McCall. A seven o'clock tee time. Are you interested?"

"No, thanks. Golf has never been of much interest to me."

"A Friday-night family potluck at the high school, then? I know you like to eat."

Sara said, "Come on, Charity. You can't miss the potluck. Terri's signed her family up for it."

"All right. I'll go to the potluck."

"Great!" Ashley exclaimed. "And you absolutely *must* be at the dance on Saturday evening. Everyone eighteen and over is going to that. Just *everyone*."

Sara reached across the table and patted the back of Charity's hand where it held the mug. "She's telling the truth. Just about everybody in these mountains who's old enough to have a diploma and is still breathing will be in the gym for the dance."

Did *everybody* mean Buck too?

She gave her head a shake, trying to dislodge the unwelcome question in her mind.

Ashley said, "I'm sorry, but I won't take no for an answer." She made a mark on the paper.

A baby's cry drifted down the stairs and into the kitchen. "Sounds like Eddy's ready to eat again." Sara pushed back her chair. "Do you both want to come up while I nurse him?"

"No, thanks," Ashley answered. "I'll run along. Maybe we can get together again next week." She closed the binder with a flourish.

Charity said, "I'll come with you, Sara." She was proud of how steady her voice was. Her pulse quickened a bit, but there was no sense of dread. That was progress.

Ashley let herself out while Sara and Charity climbed the stairs to the master bedroom. Eddy's cries sounded more demanding with each passing moment. Sara went straight to the cradle and picked him up, then carried him to the rocking chair.

"Isn't he beautiful?" she asked, her gaze fastened on the infant.

Charity took several steps toward her. "Yes, Sara. He's beautiful." And he was.

"A Malone through and through. Look at that square jaw. Just like his daddy's."

And like his uncle too.

BUCK AND SHERIFF LESTER STUDIED THE SIGNS LEFT behind by the bear. Only one set of prints. No cubs following after an adult female. And the tracks led away from Kings Meadow proper. Good news.

Still, folks had been alerted to a bear's presence in the area—one neighbor passing along the news to another by phone or on the street. The bear hadn't been sighted. More than likely, it had returned to the mountains soon after its encounter with Cocoa. Perhaps even nursing a few wounds of its own. Buck considered himself lucky. The bear had traveled right through the middle of his acreage. Bears usually left horses alone, but if Cocoa had been in pursuit, it might have struck out at anything in its path.

After the sheriff left, Buck stayed outside, hoping to work off some of his restless energy. He started by mucking out the covered lean-to. The physical labor felt good, and it was the kind of work that allowed his thoughts to wander. No surprise that they wandered to Charity. Images of her flooded his mind. So many it seemed he'd been collecting them for years instead of weeks, each one of them meaningful to him. Some made him want to laugh with her, some to cry for her. Some should have made him angry, he supposed, but they didn't.

Summer was flying by. If he wanted to win her heart, he'd best hurry before he ran out of time. It would become more difficult, if not impossible, once she was back in Boise.

He wasn't certain how much time had passed before he heard the crunch of tires. He looked up in time to see Charity's Lexus stop in the Anderson driveway. He set aside the pitchfork and headed toward the neighboring house, wiping away the sweat with a hand towel. Charity got out of her SUV and had already entered the backyard before she saw his approach. She waited on the other side of the closed gate.

It felt more like a wall between them.

"How's Cocoa?" he asked when he stopped a couple of yards away.

"Dr. Parry wants to keep her at the clinic for a day or two. To make sure there's no infection. But she seems to be doing all right."

"Glad to hear it." He gave her a sympathetic smile. "And what about you? How are you holding up?"

She was silent for a few moments. Finally, she said, "I'm good too."

Instinct told Buck to give her some time and space. He took a step back. "Well, I've got more chores to do. Better get to them. You'll be sure and let me know if there's anything I can do for you or Cocoa. Right?"

She nodded.

"Okay, then. See you later." With a tip of his head, he turned on his heel and headed back to the work that awaited him.

But his thoughts—and his heart—remained with Charity.

Chapter 21

WHEN THE TELEPHONE RANG ON SATURDAY, A LITTLE before noon, Charity ignored it. She'd brought Cocoa home from the vet's earlier that morning, and she'd been writing up a storm for the past two and a half hours while her faithful companion slept nearby. She didn't want to break the flow while it was going so well. Whoever was calling would simply have to leave a message or try again later.

Charity's dystopian-set Lancer Series featured a strong, smart, courageous female protagonist named Ghleanna. While there were some good—even heroic—male characters in those books, there was never more than a hint of a potential romantic relationship with Ghleanna. Charity's former editor had loved the books that way. So had Charity.

But, to her surprise, she'd warmed to the developing romances in her new novel. And she was as fond of her secondary teenaged couple as she was of her slightly more mature hero and heroine, two people about the same age as Charity herself.

And the same age as Buck.

She closed her eyes and sighed. She hadn't meant to let her neighbor sneak into her thoughts. Not again. Not today. Not when she needed to stay focused on her story. She might as well have answered the phone. Nobody else could disturb her the way Buck Malone could. Even when he didn't try to. Even when he wasn't present.

She looked at her laptop screen and poised her fingers over the keyboard. Then she waited. And waited. Nothing. Not a word. Not a single noun or verb or adjective. Not any narrative or dialogue. Nothing. Like a river that had been dammed by the sudden collapse of a mountainside.

"Go away, Buck."

Cocoa raised her head.

"Ignore me, girl. I'm okay." She rose from the desk, closing the laptop as she did so. "Let's eat something."

Charity went to the sheepskin-lined dog bed and lifted Cocoa into her arms. Once down the stairs, she set Cocoa on the floor and allowed the dog to limp her way into the kitchen. It made Charity's chest ache to see her faithful pal like this. What if the bear had killed her? What if Buck hadn't found her in time?

Buck again.

Standing in the kitchen, the memory of the kiss they'd shared in this room came rushing back. Tingling sensations shot through her, and her breath became short. The kiss had been more than she'd dreamed any kiss could be.

How did I let it happen?

She released a sigh as she opened the refrigerator. Stood there a short while looking until, undecided on what to eat, she finally closed the door. That was when she noticed the blinking light on the answering machine. She went to it and punched the Play button.

"Hi, Charity." Nathan's voice. "Sorry I missed you. About me coming up tomorrow. Looks like I won't make it. My boss is sending me out of town for the next week, and I'll be thirty thousand feet in the air at noon tomorrow. I'm really sorry. How about I call you once I'm settled in the hotel? Should be around four or so, Mountain Time. Hope you'll be near the phone then. Take care."

Click.

Nathan's kisses had never made her feel the way Buck's one brief kiss had. And as that realization swept over her, she also knew that she and Nathan would never get back together again. She didn't love him. If she was honest with herself, she'd known it wouldn't work when he'd come to see her last Sunday.

No, I knew the day he first called.

She was moving on. She was getting better, stronger. She wasn't going to settle for something less. She might not be ready yet, but she would get there.

BUCK ARRIVED AT HIS BROTHER'S HOME A LITTLE before five. He'd been invited to join the family for dinner, an opportunity he tried never to pass up. And being there would give him some time with the newest member of the Malone clan. Little Eddy had completely captured his uncle's heart.

"Wow, Sara," he said after embracing his sister-in-law. "You look more beautiful every time I see you. Being a mother of four agrees with you."

She laughed. "You're a charming liar, Buck Malone. My hair is a disaster, and I haven't lost an ounce that I gained while pregnant. But thanks anyway."

"My brother isn't lying," Ken said as he draped an arm over his wife's shoulders. "You do look more beautiful each day."

She feigned a frown. "Are you trying to get out of doing the dishes when dinner's over?"

"Maybe," Ken and Buck answered in unison, both grinning.

"Uh-huh." She shook her head but returned their smiles.

"Where's Eddy?" Buck asked.

"In the family room." Ken looked at Sara. "You go on with him. I'll keep an eye on the stove."

"Thanks, hon."

Sara led the way down the hall. A kind of ordered chaos ruled the family room. Buck found it appealing. Krista and Sharon played a board game on the floor near the sliding glass door that led onto the patio. Their brother Jake played a video game on the large-screen television. In a bassinet near the sofa, Eddy slept, blissfully unaware of the invaders from outer space being blown to bits on the screen.

Buck glanced at Sara, and after she nodded, he scooped up the infant. "He's going to look like you."

"Are you joking? He's a Malone through and through. In fact, I said those very same words to Charity a couple of days ago."

He looked up from the baby but tried not to sound too interested. "Is that right?"

"Mmm. She came over after checking on her dog at the vet's. Ashley was here, too, and before Ash left, she made certain Charity signed up for both the reunion potluck and the dance."

Buck settled on the sofa, and Sara sat beside him, smiling as she looked at her baby.

"Must be a huge relief, how well Eddy's doing."

"I can't begin to say."

"How old is he? I've already lost track."

"Five weeks yesterday." Sara reached out and lightly touched the tip of his tiny nose.

Buck looked at his sister-in-law. "Did Charity tell you how upset she got the day Eddy was born? I guess she was afraid you or the baby wouldn't make it. She ran out of the waiting area like the place was on fire."

"No," Sara answered, eyes growing wide. "She didn't tell me."

"I was worried about her, but she wouldn't talk about it when she came back."

Sara straightened and leaned back from him, as if to get a better look at his face. "Something's changed about you."

"About me? Nah. I'm the same."

She released a soft gasp. "It's Charity, isn't it?"

"What about Charity?"

"You like her. And more than just a little too."

He looked down at his infant nephew and felt a tug in his heart toward a different future than he used to envision for himself. One that needed a wider circle to contain all of the people he loved. One worth having, even with the risk.

Chapter 22

Buck and the Ultimate Adventures guests turned back from their trail ride when dark-gray clouds blew in from the south. Storms out of the south, Buck knew, were usually bad news. This time was no exception. While the small group was still fifteen minutes from the barn, the sky opened up and dropped rain on them in heavy sheets. In an instant they were soaked through to the skin, and there wasn't anything they could do except ride on.

The weather report hadn't called for rain. If it had, Buck would have tied rain slickers to the back of each saddle or canceled the ride altogether. But the reports had called for a clear and sunny day. Since clear and sunny were what residents of Kings Meadow enjoyed for most of the summer months, Buck hadn't had reason to expect anything different.

He reined in and turned his gelding off the trail. "Sorry, folks," he called to the party of six. "We're almost there." He hunched his shoulders against the downpour. Water ran off the brim of his hat as if from a faucet. "Just keep headed in that direction." He pointed with his arm. "Sorry it's so miserable."

He waited until the last guest had passed him, then turned his horse onto the trail again. It was hard to see, and the last thing he needed was to lose somebody in the storm.

Chet and Kimberly were waiting for them in the barn. Kimberly passed out towels and, when the guests were ready to put something in their hands, large mugs of hot chocolate. Chet helped Buck tend to the horses. By the time the men were finished, the guests had been driven back to their quarters.

"Rotten thing to have happen," Chet said.

Buck rubbed his hair with the towel he'd used earlier. "Hope your guests don't blame you for the weather."

"You can never tell." Chet shrugged. "You know how it is."

"Yeah, I know. Most of the folks I work with are great. They love the outdoors and horses, and they take in stride whatever comes while on a trip. But every so often . . ." Buck let his words fade into silence as he gave his head a slow shake.

Chet grunted in response.

Buck looked toward the open barn door. "It's not letting up."

"We need the moisture. Been a dry summer." Chet leaned his shoulder against a post. "Buck, when do you think you'll go back to outfitting?"

"I don't have anything booked until the end of August."

"How'd you like to come work for me until then? Full time. Not just leading trail rides for our guests but training horses, too, and general ranch work. I could really use you."

Buck didn't have to think about the offer. "Chet, there's

nothing I'd like better. I'm not used to having a lot of spare time on my hands. I like to be busy."

"Great. Start tomorrow morning?"

"Sure," he said. "I'll be here. Eight o'clock? Or do you want me earlier?"

"Eight's fine." Chet grinned. "Kimberly's going to be glad to hear it. She's been after me to hire another hand ever since Denny left for Colorado. I haven't been very happy with the interviews I've had. Then I started wondering about you. You know horses and ranch work, and you're good with people too. You're a perfect fit."

"I'll try not to disappoint you."

"I'm not worried about that." Chet slapped a hand on Buck's shoulder. "Only disappointment will be when you leave us."

Chet's words stayed with Buck during the drive home. It felt good, the trust the other man had shown in him. What was more surprising was how much he liked the idea of ranch work. Especially the horse-training part. He knew a lot, but he didn't know as much as Chet Leonard. Nobody in these mountains knew as much as Chet. A paycheck, even for a single month, would be a big help. Learning more about horse training from Chet would be a major bonus.

As his truck approached his driveway, the rain—little more than a sprinkle now—stopped and the clouds broke apart, letting through a bright beam of sunlight. It felt like a promise of some kind. Almost as a response, Charity sprang to mind. And along with her image came an old Vince Gill song. He began to sing it to himself. The lyrics were perfect. They described exactly how Charity made him feel.

Whenever she came around, she made his knees go weak and his breath catch. Her smile turned his world upside down.

But he wouldn't keep his feelings hidden. That part of the song was all wrong. Buck Malone was more determined than that. He just needed to find the right moment.

CLAD IN HER COTTON PAJAMAS, CHARITY STAYED UP until midnight in order to Skype with her parents at eight in the morning in Rome.

"Hi, Mom. Hi, Dad." She leaned closer to the laptop screen. "How are you? You look fabulous."

"Thanks, honey," her mom replied. "We are good. You cannot believe all of the wonderful things we've seen and the marvelous people we've met. I know we say that every time we talk, but it's so true. We *are* having the trip of a lifetime."

"Are you going to be ready to come home at the end of the month?"

"Of course. Dorothy was right, you know. There's no place like home. But that doesn't mean we won't enjoy every single moment we're here."

Charity laughed softly.

"Now, tell us. How are you? How's the book coming?"

"I'm okay, and the book's coming along great. I'll finish on time, and I think I'll really like the book when it's done."

Sophie Anderson repositioned her iPad. "You look a little tired. Are you getting enough sleep?"

"Yes, Mom. I'm getting enough sleep."

"Don't poke your chin out, dear. I'm still your mother and I worry about you."

Charity gave her head a small shake. "I know, Mom, but you don't have to worry."

She imagined her sister pointing a finger at her, telling her that their mom did have cause to worry. And with it came a shiver in her stomach. When her parents returned, she would have to tell them everything she'd told Terri. At least with her sister, it had been over the phone. She wouldn't get that same distance when she shared everything with her mom and dad. It was going to be harder than she wanted to contemplate.

The iPad got pulled over so that her dad's face was all she saw. "My turn," he said, looking at her mom offscreen. Then he smiled at Charity before asking, "How's Cocoa?"

"Pretty good, considering. She's getting around on three legs without trouble. She still sleeps a lot, but I think that's the pain meds the vet has me give her."

"Did the bear show up again?"

"No. No sightings anywhere. Must have gone back to the mountains right after it met up with Cocoa."

"Well, that's a relief. I hate it when a wild animal has to be shot just because it comes too close to civilization. It was only doing what bears do." He frowned at her. "But you be careful when you're outside, all the same."

"I will."

"How's your house coming along?"

"Good, I think. Although the contractor is pretty tight-lipped about progress when I talk to him on the phone. I plan to drive down to Boise one day this week to see for myself."

Charity's mom popped back into view, going cheek to cheek with her husband. "Honey, we've got to go. We're signed up for a tour this morning, and we don't want to miss the bus."

"Okay. Have a great time. Love you!"

"We'll talk again next week. Bye. Love you too."

The Skype connection was broken, and Charity felt the emptiness of the house swirl around her as she closed her laptop. After a few moments, she unfolded her legs, got up from the bed, and returned the computer to the desk. A breeze fluttered the curtains over the window, and she went to lower it about halfway before switching off the bedside lamp. Outside the night was pitch-black, clouds hiding the moon and stars. No lights were on at Buck's house. Now that he was up and mobile, she'd learned that he was an early-to-bed, early-to-rise guy.

She lay down and pulled the sheet and lightweight blanket up to her chin. But she didn't close her eyes. If she did, she knew thoughts about Buck would inevitably lead her back to the kiss they'd shared. Time and space hadn't helped her forget it. The memory was always close by. It took great willpower to keep it at bay. Sometimes she succeeded. Often she did not.

It would be good for her to get away from Kings Meadow for a day. She'd already planned to go down to Boise to meet with the contractor and see the progress on her house. She would do it tomorrow or Wednesday. She would return to the valley and see how it felt to be home again.

Chapter 23

BUCK STARED AT THE FLAT TIRE, THEN AT THE USE-less jack. He couldn't believe his bad luck. Who knew how long it would be before someone stopped to offer help? Traffic was sparse this early on a weekday morning. It would pick up later, but he might as well settle in for a wait.

The truck belonged to Chet Leonard's sons. Chet had asked Buck to drive it down to the valley to pick up a special piece of equipment. He should have been able to complete the errand in under four hours—if not for a flat tire and a broken hydraulic jack. He should have brought his own truck. It might not look this good, but at least he knew his jack was in working order. Something teenagers didn't always think about.

He looked north, up the winding two-lane highway. He could see about a quarter mile before a bend in the road hid any oncoming traffic. Looking south got an almost identical view.

Might as well get comfortable.

He dropped the tailgate and hopped onto it. At least it wasn't hot yet, and there was a nice breeze off the river. He should be able to hitch a ride to the nearest public phone before the temperature climbed above eighty.

He bumped the brim of his hat with his knuckles. He hoped this incident wouldn't mess up his day so badly he'd have to cancel his dance lesson with Skye. He looked forward to it. He'd realized that the all-class reunion dance would be his best chance to sweep Charity off her feet. Cliché, perhaps, but that was what he intended to do.

He wondered if she'd noticed his absence the last couple of days. He wondered if she thought about him at all. He hoped so. Remembering the night he'd kissed her, remembering the night she'd kissed him back, he had convinced himself she cared for him. At least a little.

If I could just get more time with her. I need a day for her and me. Like the day we went riding . . . only better.

The thought had barely become conscious when a light-colored SUV rounded the bend from the north. It couldn't be. But it was.

Charity.

Buck dropped off the tailgate and lifted his arm to wave her down. There was a moment when he wondered if she would stop—she wouldn't recognize the truck—but then he saw the Lexus slow down. She brought the automobile to a halt a couple of yards behind the pickup.

Buck approached the driver's side door as she lowered the window. "Are you a sight for sore eyes," he said.

"What's happened? Whose truck is that?"

"Flat tire. Belongs to Chet's boys. I'm supposed to pick

up some ranch equipment down in Boise, but the hydraulic jack is broken. Don't suppose you have one of those for this rig of yours?" He tried to make the question sound teasing.

She shook her head, her expression serious.

"Can you give me a lift? There's a pay phone at the café a few miles from here. I can call Chet and then walk back to the truck to wait for him."

"I wouldn't make you walk." She motioned with her head. "Get in."

He moved swiftly to the passenger's side of the car, opened the door, removed his hat, and slipped in. The interior was as luxurious as the name Lexus promised consumers. He hadn't taken any note of it on the day Eddy was born. Now he did.

"Nice," he said, glancing into the backseat.

She sounded almost apologetic when she answered, "It was my one big splurge after my books took off. Well, it and my house."

I could never afford to buy you anything like it. The thought made his gut clench.

Charity restarted the engine, checked for traffic, then pulled onto the highway. Neither spoke in the short time it took to reach the café overlooking the river. Once there, Charity parked her car near the restaurant's entrance. The public phone was inside the doors and to the right.

"I'll wait for you," she said as he opened the car door.

"Thanks."

Kimberly answered the phone. Buck quickly explained the situation, then she asked him to hold on. He waited.

It took awhile before Chet's voice came over the wire. He

asked a few questions, then said, "This is Sam's responsibility, Buck, and he's going to have to take care of it. But he's not here right now. You stay put and I'll come get you."

The idea came to him, sudden and perfect. "Hey, boss. I know I've just started working for you full-time but . . . do you think I could take some time off?"

Silence greeted him from the other end of the line.

"I was hoping maybe I could ride along with Charity. She's the one who gave me a lift."

Chet laughed. "Kimberly told me you were sweet on Charity, but I didn't believe her. Guess she was right. You go on. I can manage without you today." He chuckled again. "Kimberly's going to love this when I tell her. See you when you get back."

Buck hung up the phone but didn't move away at once. He still needed to figure out what to say to Charity. He couldn't lie, but he didn't want this to blow up in his face either. He would have to choose his words carefully.

CHARITY CLICKED HER FINGERNAILS AGAINST THE steering wheel in time with the music playing on the stereo. She didn't feel impatient. Her appointment with the contractor wasn't until early in the afternoon. She had plenty of time before then.

From the corner of her eye, she saw the restaurant door swing open. Buck appeared and strode toward her in that easy gait of his, coming to a stop beside her door. She turned down the volume of the music as she glanced up at him.

"Well, I talked to Chet," Buck said, "and there's a problem."

She raised her eyebrows.

"Chet wants Sam to take care of this since it was his responsibility. But Sam isn't around right now. Won't be for a few hours. I didn't want to ask you to drive me back to Kings Meadow, and I hate for Chet to have to drive out here twice in one day. Once for me. Once to bring Sam. So I thought, if you don't mind, I'd tag along with you down to Boise. I'd buy you lunch." He ended with a questioning grin. A completely charming, devastatingly handsome grin.

Her heart flip-flopped in her chest. A day in Boise with Buck Malone. Why did that sound almost like a date?

"Unless, of course, I'd be in the way."

"No, I . . . It would be fine. Of course you can come. Get in."

Buck strode around to the opposite side and opened the passenger door once again. Charity had to force herself not to watch his every movement. Once he was seated beside her and seat-belted in, she started the engine and steered the car back onto the highway.

Driving along this stretch of river was one of her favorite things to do. Whenever she came up to see her parents, this was what she looked forward to first. She loved the climb out of the valley, the falling away of sagebrush and foothills, the first sign of pine trees and clear running water. The beauty of nature all around made her heart sing. She'd had her reasons for staying away from Kings Meadow, but this wasn't one of them.

As if reading her thoughts, Buck said, "God didn't hold back when He created Idaho, did He?"

She smiled, liking his comment, though her attention remained on the winding road ahead.

"So what's taking you to Boise?"

"My house. I want to see how the renovations are coming along."

"Hey, that's great. I'd love to see where you live. The way we live says a lot about us, don't you think?"

"Yes. I suppose it does." She felt his gaze upon her and for some reason feared she might blush.

"So what does my place say about me?" he asked.

"Confirmed bachelor?"

"Ouch."

The response surprised her. "Isn't that what you want it to say about you?" *Isn't that what you are?*

"It's who I've been up to now. But I'm always open to change. I think this summer has changed me. Hopefully for the better."

An odd feeling thrummed inside her chest. She wished she understood what it meant.

They fell into silence as the road and river parted ways and the pine trees were left behind. Another fifteen minutes and they reached the valley.

Breaking the silence, Charity said, "My appointment with the contractor isn't until this afternoon. Shall we have an early lunch?"

"Sure, sounds good."

She had a favorite restaurant that overlooked the Boise River. At this point in the summer they would be sure to see lots of people floating by in inner tubes and rafts. It was a popular activity in hot weather. Her home was about half-way between the launching point at Barber Dam and the exit point at Ann Morrison Park, and she had a fine view in her tree-shaded yard from where she could watch people enjoy-ing the river. Not just in the summer when they were on the water but year-round as they walked and bicycled and skated along the Greenbelt that followed the river for miles and miles and miles.

As was true for many who chose to live and work in Idaho's capital city, Charity loved nature and thrived on activities in the outdoors. At the same time, she loved being able to attend the Idaho Shakespeare Festival or get tickets to a Broadway show. Not to mention the ballet and the philharmonic orches-tra. And there was a little thing called BSU football that had become her passion as well.

She glanced over at Buck, wondering if he would care for any of the cultural activities she loved about the city. Or would he be the proverbial fish out of water in a place like this? Was he the type of cowboy who only cared about horses and the wilderness? Or did he have other sides to him she'd never seen?

Such questions were still swirling in her head when they arrived at the restaurant. Almost before the engine died, Buck was out of the car and coming around to open the door for her. If she knew nothing else about him, she knew he'd been raised to be a gentleman.

The restaurant was a popular placed to have lunch, but they were early enough to beat the crowd. They had their pick of seating outdoors at one of the shaded tables.

"Have you been here before?" she asked as she sat on the chair he held for her.

"Nope." He rounded the small table to sit directly oppo-site her. "Looks nice."

"The food is great, but what I like most is the view. I've

always loved our rivers. The water runs so clean and clear. I was surprised when I started to travel more and learned it isn't like that everywhere."

Buck smiled at her, and as had happened before, she felt it all the way to her toes. Was she going to blush again?

The waitress came to their table—a welcome interruption—and Charity ordered a Cobb salad with Thousand Island dressing on the side. Buck asked for the same.

Shouts of laughter carried to them from the river. They looked up to see the inhabitants of two rafts splashing one another with their oars. Teenagers, it looked like. Three boys and three girls in each raft.

Buck chuckled. "Remember when we were that young and carefree?"

She smiled at him. "Yes, I remember."

She was surprised to realize she meant it. For years now, all of her memories had been tainted by that one winter's night in the Riverton mansion. But sitting here with Buck, it was as if a cool breeze had blown a thousand lies and regrets away.

Chapter 24

FOR A CHANGE, BUCK FELT AS IF HE'D SAID SOME-
thing right to Charity. As if he'd said something that pleased
her. He hoped he could repeat it.

He would be the first to admit that he didn't always
understand women. He liked them and they seemed to like
him. But liking didn't mean understanding. Until Charity, he
hadn't felt much of a desire to improve his understanding. It
had seemed too much of an investment of time for the short-
term relationships he'd preferred. Now things were different.
He wanted to know Charity. Really *know* her.

Their Cobb salads arrived. Charity invited him to bless
the food, and he obliged. As they began eating, Buck asked
about her parents. She seemed to enjoy relating the news of
what they'd seen and done. And since he liked to hear it, it was
a good way to pass the meal.

When they finished eating, Buck paid the bill and they
went outside to her car.

"We'll get to the house before the contractor," she said, "but I can show you around while we wait for him."

"I'd like that." As he'd told her earlier, he was curious to see her home, to see her in it.

They drove along city streets and through shaded neighborhoods. Buck knew the main thoroughfares of Boise, but he had no idea where they were by the time Charity slowed her Lexus, except that they were somewhere near the river.

"There it is," she said, pointing with her right hand.

Buck saw the large Victorian home up ahead. Painted in two tones of gray, it had a porch that wrapped around the sides and front. Peaks and turrets accented the second and third stories and the roof. "It's got character," he said.

A smile could be heard in her voice. "You see it too?"

"Yeah. It fits you."

She laughed. "That's what I thought the instant the Realtor showed it to me. It looks like my house. Feels like my house. I'll be glad when the renovations are done. I have no idea what we'll find inside."

A big white truck was parked in the driveway, so Charity pulled to the curb and turned off the engine. Once they were both out of the car, she led the way to the front door. It was unlocked.

"Hello? Mr. Tompkins? Are you here?"

No one answered.

"Everyone must be at lunch," Charity said. "Come on. I'll give you the grand tour."

She didn't exaggerate. It was a grand tour, as far as Buck was concerned, despite the construction still in progress on the main floor and the sheets that covered most of the furniture.

It was a home built for the large families that had been common in the 1800s. Many bedrooms. Several sitting areas. A wood-paneled library. The old-world charm of the house remained, despite the improvements and modernizations.

"I converted the top floor into my office when I first bought the place," Charity said as she led the way to the third story. "There were quite a few smaller rooms up here. Servants' quarters when the house was built."

Buck turned a corner in the narrow staircase, and suddenly he was facing a large, open room with a bank of ceiling-to-floor windows. A wooden desk and credenza, their surfaces also covered in white sheets, were at the far right-hand corner of the room. Bookcases lined the wall to his left.

He walked to the windows. "Wow." The southern-exposed room looked out upon an emerald-green lawn, tall trees, and a clear view of the river flowing by.

"I lost most of my flower gardens in the flood." Charity stepped up beside him. "But the lawn came back better than I expected, and I didn't lose any trees. And before long, the house will be back in order too."

It's beautiful, but it's . . . sterile. Was that the word he wanted? He'd said a house told something about the person who lived in it. This one spoke volumes to him about Charity. Despite its beauty and all of her considerable efforts, it didn't feel like a home.

"I hear someone downstairs," Charity said, intruding on his thoughts. "It must be Mr. Tompkins. Feel free to look around some more while I talk to him." She left the office.

Buck continued to stare out the window.

He knew something about trying to avoid pain by

avoiding love. It seemed to him Charity had tried to do the same. But at least he had people around him, close friends and neighbors. Charity had taken herself away from the community she'd known as a girl and, from what he could tell, hadn't tried to make a new one here.

He would like to be the first member of her new community. He would like to be the man who helped her make this house—or any other she might choose—into a home.

By the time Charity finished talking to her contractor, the workmen had returned from lunch. Machines buzzed. Hammers pounded. It wouldn't take long before a headache developed from the noise. Which reminded her to be thankful she had a quiet place to retreat to for these final weeks of renovating and remodeling.

She found Buck at the edge of her property, watching the Boise River flow by. Shaded by the trees, he had removed his hat and was twirling it with the fingers of his right hand. More people in rafts and tubes bobbed past him. Even a small dog in a miniature raft of its own—clad in a doggie life jacket with a kind of handle on its back—floated down the center of the river, tied to the owner's larger raft.

When she stopped at Buck's side, he said, amusement in his voice, "Does Cocoa have a special raft and life jacket?"

The question made her laugh with him. "No."

"People are kind of entertaining to watch, aren't they?"

"Usually."

"Not exactly whitewater rafting. Not like our river up home."

Our river. The words sounded sweet. *Up home.*

"No," she said again with a shake of her head. "This section of the Boise River is too peaceful for that. Two or three short falls to go over and a few spots of minor rapids. But nothing scary. Unless you let yourself get caught in branches along the banks. That can be dangerous."

"Maybe I should try it sometime."

Now why did that cause her heart to flutter? "Maybe you should."

"Will you go with me?" He looked at her, the curves at the corners of his mouth hinting at a smile.

"Sure." Her heart did more than flutter this time. It raced, making her breathless and dizzy. "If the weather's still hot enough when I finish my book, we could go then."

"Count on it, Charity." He grinned in earnest.

Ka-thump-ka-thump-ka-thump.

He tipped his head slightly to one side as he studied her with his eyes. Finally, he asked, "Are you finished inside?"

"Yes. I'm finished."

"Maybe we should start for home."

There was that word again. *Home.* His home in Kings Meadow. Her home in Boise. Her gaze slipped to the back of the house, and she suddenly felt frightened. Frightened over a choice she might have to make.

And even more frightened that a choice might never be needed.

Buck's hand lightly cupped her elbow, and they fell into step, crossing the lawn to the side gate, then walking out to the curb where Charity had parked the car. As before, he accompanied her to the driver's side and held the door for her. Before she slid into her seat, she looked up at him and, for a moment, wondered if he might lean down and kiss her. But he didn't.

Just as well, she told herself, though she didn't believe it.

Neither of them spoke as they drove away from her house and through town. But once they were on the highway headed north, Buck broke the silence.

"So tell me. Besides writing books, playing with Cocoa, and watching rafters on the river, what do you do with yourself in Boise? No horseback riding. You already told me that."

She thought about it before answering. "I love to cook. I'm really looking forward to getting into my new kitchen. I like to bike along the Greenbelt in the summer. I love to attend the theater and ballet. Mom taught me to knit, but I'm not very good at it. Dad taught me to love old movies, and that's what I usually watch on television. Oh, and I enjoy fishing." She glanced over at him. "What about you?"

"Horses and dogs and pretty much anything in nature. Spending time with family and friends. Helping them out when they need it. Studying the Bible with the men's group I'm part of." He paused for a few moments, then added, "I like to dance when I get the chance."

It struck her that almost everything she'd mentioned was an activity she did alone. The things he'd mentioned were activities he did with others.

"*You* like to dance," he added softly.

"How do you know that?"

"I watched you dancing on the Fourth. You were having a great time."

He watches me. No. More than that. He sees me.

The pleasure that cascaded through her was undeniable, as well as surprising. Surprising because she'd spent the last decade trying to hide the girl inside, and yet happiness had come when someone looked beneath the surface. Buck had looked and seen.

He sees me. He doesn't know my secrets, but somehow he still sees me.

As Charity drove toward Kings Meadow, she felt God heal another broken piece inside her heart.

SKYE FOSTER GRINNED AS SHE TURNED AWAY FROM the CD player, the studio silent once again. "You are definitely ready for the reunion," she said to Buck. "The gals will be fighting to dance with you there."

"Not exactly what I'm after."

Her smile broadened. "I know that. You're doing this for Charity, and I think that's real romantic. If you two get married, I want to give both of you lessons for your first dance as husband and wife. Deal?"

Marriage to Charity. He liked the sound of it—and that continued to surprise him when he thought of it—but it could be a long shot. Despite the way today had turned out, despite the good time they'd had down in Boise and the things they'd talked about during the drive down and back, she still didn't seem ready to open up and let Buck all the way into her life. He might love her. She might even care for him. But he wanted more than to win her love. He needed her to trust him. Trust him with everything. He needed answers that only she could give him. Why had she become so upset at the hospital the day Sara gave birth to Eddy? Why had she gone so pale at the sight of the Riverton mansion on the day of their ride? Why could she be so warm and approachable one moment, then cool and untouchable the next?

"Hey, Buck. Are you all right?"

He blinked, bringing Skye back into focus. "Sorry. Yeah, I'm good." He motioned with his head toward the door. "Guess it's time for me to get on home."

"Wait. Before you go. I hear you're working out at the Leonard Ranch now. How're you liking that?"

"Like it fine. Why?"

"I was thinking about offering line dance lessons to their Ultimate Adventures guests. Think anybody'd be interested?"

"Might be. Couldn't hurt to ask. The Leonards give out all kinds of flyers and brochures to their guests. Whitewater rafting. Horseback riding. Mountain biking. Why not line dancing?" He shrugged.

"I'll do it. I'll put together a brochure as soon as I get home tonight. Thanks."

With a touch of his fingers to his hat brim, Buck turned and left the studio. As he walked to his pickup truck, he wondered if his advice to Skye wasn't what he needed to hear himself: couldn't hurt to ask.

It was time he asked the right sort of questions and gave Charity a chance to answer.

Chapter 25

THE FRIENDLY BEAN HAD OPENED EARLIER IN THE summer in a converted house a half block off Main Street. From what Charity had heard, the new coffee shop had become one of the most popular places in town. Judging by how busy it was on a weekday morning, that was obviously true.

There were a half dozen tables with umbrellas on the side patio outside the coffee shop. All but one of them was occupied. Charity bought herself a latte and carried it to the available table.

Why haven't I done this before?

She glanced around, and when her gaze met with others she knew, she smiled and nodded.

That's why. I was hiding from people who would know me.

Odd, wasn't it? How that desire to isolate had taken over her life. Even when she'd been at parties or in other small groups, she'd kept herself hidden behind a carefully constructed façade. Her public persona as a novelist was as great a fiction as anything she'd written in her books.

Hiding her true self was easy in Boise. It wasn't as easy in Kings Meadow. Which was, perhaps, the real reason she'd spent most of her time this summer alone in her parents' house. But not today.

Buck would be proud of me if he knew.

Midge Foster walked over to her table. "Morning, Charity. Haven't seen you here before."

"This is my first time." She lifted her cup a little higher. "They make great coffee. I should have come sooner."

"We'll see you at the reunion, won't we?"

"Yes, I'll be there."

Midge glanced at her wristwatch. "Oh, heavens. I've got to run. My first appointment is in ten minutes." She fluttered her fingers in farewell and walked away at a brisk pace.

Charity took a few sips of her latte. Then Mayor Abbott came to say hello. He asked about her parents, said he was looking forward to her next book, then hurried off in the direction of his office. She smiled as she watched him go. Ollie Abbott would make a colorful character in a book. One of those secondary characters who tried to steal the show from the protagonists.

"Charity?"

She glanced toward the voice. It belonged to Ashley Holloway.

"Mind if I join you? It's the only available chair outside."

"Be my guest."

Ashley sat down, then swept her free-flowing hair over her shoulder. Unlike Charity, she had never tried to hide herself away. Ashley exuded self-confidence and accepted her popularity as her due. She looked around at the other tables, waved and smiled at people she knew, then finally returned her eyes to Charity.

"I can't believe how much work this reunion has been," she said. "This morning my husband asked me if we needed to buy a second home here." She laughed, the sound light and airy.

Charity smiled. "It'll be over soon. Only another week."

"You know the best part, Charity? Talking to everybody, especially those who don't live here anymore. Did you know one of our old classmates is on a long-term mission in Africa? Something to do with doctors or surgeons or something."

Charity shook her head.

"And yesterday you'll never guess who I managed to track down."

She responded as she was expected to. "Who?"

"Jon Riverton. And I may have convinced him to come to the reunion. At least he said he'd think about it. Can you believe it?"

Ashley kept talking, but Charity had stopped listening, her smile frozen in place. Her pulse raced. Her mind buzzed. Her lungs were sucked dry of oxygen. She hadn't expected this reaction. Not again. Not after she'd told her secret to Terri. Not after she'd been working so hard to understand her emotions, to discover why she'd allowed one night to shape her whole life. She'd thought she was making progress.

She stood. "Ashley, I'm sorry. I remembered something I must do, and I'm late. Please forgive me."

Cut off in mid-sentence, Ashley looked at her with a

surprised expression, but Charity didn't wait to hear a reply. She spun away from the table and hurried toward the parking lot across the street.

BUCK HELD UP A LEVEL TO THE FOUR-BY-FOUR POST that stood in a hole Ken had dug for it. "Where'd you say Sara got the plans for this swing set?"

"On Pinterest, I think. Or maybe it was on one of those home-improvement shows she likes to watch."

"Did she choose the color?"

"Uh-huh."

"Pilots will be able to pick out your house from thirty thousand feet. It's like a beacon."

The brothers laughed.

Sara's voice intruded. "If you're making fun of the fluorescent-orange paint, you're not going to like what I fix you for lunch."

Buck and Ken stopped laughing at once, then turned sheepish looks in Sara's direction. But she couldn't hold back her own laughter, and soon the men lost control again.

"I don't care what you say," Sara said when she caught her breath. "I *like* the color, and the kids are going to love it." She held out two large plastic glasses of ice water. "Here. Drink this before you expire from dehydration."

It seemed as good an excuse as any to sit on the grass in the shade of the tree. So that's what Buck did. Ken and Sara joined him there.

Sara tipped her head back and gazed at the sky. "Buck, did I hear that you're taking dance lessons from Sky Foster?"

Buck hadn't tried to keep that bit of news a secret, but he hadn't planned to broadcast it either. "Don't know what you heard."

"Ha!" She looked at him. "So it's true?"

He shrugged. "Yeah, it's true."

"Do you have a date you're taking to the reunion, by any chance?"

"No."

"Mmm." Sara gave him a searching look. "I thought maybe you would have asked someone by now."

It was his turn to look at the sky. "To be honest, I've wanted to. I just . . . I haven't found the right opportunity." He glanced back at Sara.

She grinned. "How hard can it be? She's staying next door to you."

"How'd you guess it was Charity I wanted to ask?"

"Woman's intuition."

"Hmm."

Ken placed a hand on Buck's shoulder, his expression sympathetic. "It's true, bro. Woman's intuition trumps anything else you can think of. Just accept it and move on."

"Buck."

He looked at his sister-in-law again.

"Stop waiting for the right opportunity. *Make* the opportunity."

Ken cleared his throat. "Maybe I'm a little slow on the uptake today, but since when have you had trouble asking a gal out? That's been second nature to you since you were a teenager. When you've wanted female companionship, you've had it."

"It's different this time," Buck answered, gaze dropping to the glass in his hand.

There was a lengthy silence before Ken said, "Well, I'll be. You're in love."

"Yeah." He drew a deep breath and released it. "I sure am."

"Then I guess you'd better do something about it."

"Like what?"

"Like make her fall in love with you too."

CHARITY PULLED THE SUITCASES FROM UNDER THE bed. She opened the first and began tossing items of clothing into it from the dresser. It didn't matter if the clothes got wrinkled. And what couldn't go into the suitcases because of careless packing she could shove into a pillowcase or garbage bag.

"You'll be glad to be home," she said to Cocoa. "Won't you? You don't care about the workmen and the noise. We'll both be happier once we're back where we belong."

Hollow words that went nowhere.

"Hey, Charity. Are you up there?"

Her heart beat ever faster as she moved toward the bedroom window. She poked her head through the opening and looked down at Buck. "I'm here."

"I've been knocking on your door."

"I . . . I'm real busy. I didn't hear."

He gave her one of those slow, warm-honey smiles. "Can I interrupt you? I'd like to talk."

I don't want to talk. I want to run away.

"Please."

She drew a deep breath. "All right. Wait there. I'll get Cocoa and bring her down. She'll enjoy being outside." Drawing back into the bedroom, she took several long, deep breaths, then looked toward the dog's bed. "Ready to go outside?"

Cocoa didn't jump up and run to the front door as she used to at that question, but she could manage the stairs now. Slow and awkward, but she could do it. However, Charity was in a hurry this time, so she lifted Cocoa in her arms and carried her down the stairs and out to the backyard, where she set her in the grass. Another deep breath and she turned to face Buck.

"Shall we sit in the shade?" She motioned toward the chairs on the covered patio.

"Sure." As he sat, Buck removed his hat. Then he held it between his knees and slowly circled the brim with his fingers.

Was he nervous? That was unlike him.

"I enjoyed being with you in Boise yesterday," he said after a lengthy silence.

She nodded, not sure what to say. Upstairs was a half-packed suitcase. Should she tell him that?

"It's crazy. I've been trying to figure out what I wanted to say to you ever since last night. I was going to try to see you this morning, but your car was gone. So I had even more time to think about it, and I still don't know what to say. I'm probably going to stumble around a bit."

Concern welled in her chest. "What is it, Buck?"

He released a humorless laugh and lowered his gaze to the hat in his hands. "I didn't expect to be this tongue-tied."

"It can't be that bad."

"It isn't bad. It's good. At least, I think it's good." He looked up. "I'm falling in love with you, Charity."

She sucked in air. Those were the last words she'd expected to hear.

"No, that isn't right. I love you already."

"You don't know me, Buck." *Yes, he does. He sees you.*

"Look, I know you've got a life in Boise, and I've got one here. I know we don't like all of the same things. It's probably best that we don't. Right? But I've got to believe we can work through all of the important differences. I want a chance to try anyway."

If you knew everything, would you still think you could love me?

"I'd like us to go to the reunion together, Charity. You and me. So everybody knows we're *together*."

Terri was wrong. She wasn't courageous. Not in the least. Buck was offering her a chance at everything she'd hoped for, everything she'd longed for, but she realized now that she hadn't the courage to accept.

"I can't go with you, Buck. I'm going home."

He straightened in his chair, his expression wary. "You mean, to Boise?"

She nodded.

"But why now? Your house isn't finished. Your book isn't finished. Your parents aren't back yet. Why go now?"

"It doesn't matter why." She stood. "I've decided it's for the best. I'm going. Today."

He rose, staring at her hard. "Does this have anything to do with what upset you that day we were at the hospital?"

It was as if she'd turned to stone on the inside. Turned into cold, hard marble. "My reasons are none of your business," she said, her voice flat.

"I *want* them to be my business. I want to take care of

you, Charity. I want to protect you and hold you when you hurt. I want—"

"Go home, Buck."

Before he could come up with another reply, she spun away from him and went inside, closing the door with finality.

She refused to acknowledge the way her heart felt as if it were cracking apart inside.

WAS THAT IT, THEN? HAD HE BEEN COMPLETELY mistaken about her feelings? That even if she didn't love him now, she'd be willing to see if she could learn to? That she'd at least be willing to give it a try?

Buck stared at the closed door for a long while. Then his gaze went to the dog, lying peacefully in the shade, not seeming to mind that her mistress had run away.

He tried to summon up anger. Hadn't he known better than to let himself care about anybody this much? It was safer to just look out for himself, safer to go no further than friendship. He could stay a bachelor for the rest of his life and be content with it. After all, he'd been content up to now.

Liar.

Maybe last year he'd believed that. Maybe last spring he'd believed it. Maybe even a few weeks ago he'd believed it. He didn't believe it any longer. Love had made that impossible. Loving Charity.

"I'm not giving up yet," he said softly. "Not yet."

Chapter 26

CHARITY STARED OUT THE WINDOWS IN HER OFFICE. There was silence in the house this morning. It was Saturday. No workmen had come to pound or drill today, but still her head ached. As if those carpenters with their hammers had moved from the downstairs to inside her head.

Her mobile phone vibrated on her desk. She ignored it, as she'd done ever since arriving home. It was probably Buck. She'd seen his name on the caller ID several times. Finally, she'd stopped looking to see who called. She couldn't bear even that.

I wish I'd never gone up there. I should have known better. I should have known it was a mistake.

She'd wanted to find love. She'd hoped for marriage. That had been a mistake too. Obviously.

The silence of the house mocked her.

She sank down to the floor and turned, leaning her back against the windowpane. The glass was warm from the sun, but Charity still felt cold. Nothing she'd tried had taken the chill from her bones, from the icy tentacles that had wrapped around her heart two days earlier. She wanted to cry. She wanted to wail. But no tears would come. She was empty. Empty of everything.

"Charity."

Had she begun to hear voices now? That sounded like Terri.

"Charity, are you up there?"

She scrambled to her feet and was standing by the time her sister appeared at the top of the stairs.

The expression on Terri's face seemed a combination of confusion and pity. "What are you doing here, sis?"

"I came home."

"To what?" Her sister motioned with her hand, taking in the large room. "This? A place where you can hide?"

Charity shook her head. "Who told you I left Kings Meadow?"

"We came for the reunion. Remember? You were supposed to be at the potluck last night. I tried to call you, but you never answered your phone."

"I'm sorry." She turned toward the bank of windows again. "I didn't want to talk to Buck. He . . . He's called several times."

Terri came to stand between her and the window, blocking her view. "He told me what he said to you."

"He doesn't know what he's talking about. He doesn't know me. He doesn't know."

"Buck isn't stupid. He knows his own heart. He loves you."

Charity shook her head again. "No. He doesn't. He can't." Her voice fell to a whisper. "I don't deserve his love, Terri."

Her sister took a step back. "Is that what this is about?" Anger entered her voice. "Are you trying to throw away happiness with both hands just because you made a bad choice when you were still a kid?"

"You don't understand." Charity's voice rose to meet her sister's, and suddenly she couldn't keep her feelings inside anymore. "You can't understand. Hate killed my baby. My hate. *My* hate." She gasped for breath. "Why would God ever want me to be happy again after I did that?"

Terri released a soft gasp and tears filled her eyes. "Oh, Charity," she whispered. "Oh, sis. Is that what you truly believe?"

Charity hadn't known she believed it until she'd said it. And now that she did, she began to weep. No sound came with the hot tears than ran down her cheeks. Just pain. Years and years and years of pain.

Her sister's arms enveloped her. "You foolish, foolish girl. No wonder you can't accept Buck's love. You haven't been able to accept God's love either. That's where we've got to start." Terri stroked Charity's hair. "It's going to be all right, Pipsqueak. You'll see. You'll see."

All Charity could do was cling to her sister and pray it was true.

Buck had just hung up the phone after leaving another message for Charity when the doorbell rang. He walked out of the kitchen, then froze in place when he saw who was on the other side of the screen door.

"Charity."

"Hi, Buck." Her eyes were puffy. Her voice sounded scratchy.

His heart ached in response.

"May I come in?"

"Sure." He stepped forward and pushed open the screen. "Come in."

"I . . . uh . . . I'm sorry I haven't returned any of your calls."

"It's all right. You're here now." He studied her expression, the fragile look in her eye. "What made you come back to Kings Meadow?"

"Terri."

He'd hoped he was the reason, but he was thankful, no matter the cause. He reached to take her lightly by the arm and draw her to the sofa. After she sat, he joined her but was prudent enough not to sit too close. She drew in a shuddery breath, and he could see that she was steeling herself to say words that were hard. Hard for her or for him?

"You said you . . . care for me," she began.

He wanted to correct her, to remind her the word he'd used was *love*.

"But you only know what I've let you know about me. I've kept secrets from everybody for a long, long time. From friends. From family." Her voice fell to a whisper. "I tried to keep my secrets from God too. But I learned that doesn't work." A humorless smile tweaked the corners of her mouth.

He nodded to show he listened. Nothing more.

"I'm going to tell you my secrets, Buck, because you deserve to know them. But I don't want you to say anything. I especially don't want you to try to tell me none of it matters to you or makes a difference. Because it might. I want to tell you and then I'm going to go home. Not to Boise but next door. I want you to think about everything I've said and to figure out what you want. I'll understand if it isn't me. Really I will."

"It can't be as bad as all that."

She offered a slight shrug.

"Okay. I'm listening."

He did listen. And his heart didn't just ache as she told him her story. It broke for her—and perhaps for them.

True to his word, Buck didn't speak. When Charity was done, she rose from the sofa, careful not to look at him—afraid she would weaken in her resolve—and left his house. The distance from his front door to the front door of her girlhood home had never seemed so far.

Terri and Rick looked up expectantly when Charity entered. She shook her head and kept moving. Across the living room, up the stairs, down the short hall, and into the bedroom. After closing the door behind her, she went to the bed and lay on it, staring at the ceiling. Time passed in a blur. Her mind was blank.

But there finally came a moment when she realized the absence of fear. It hadn't gone into a corner, waiting to appear again. It was gone. Whatever happened in the future, the fear was gone.

A rap sounded at the door, then Terri poked her head into the room. "Ready for company?"

Charity nodded.

Terri entered and sat on the other bed. "Are you okay?"

"Yes," she answered softly. "At least, I will be."

Just as softly, Terri said, "I can see that."

They sat in silence for a long while. A comforting silence between sisters who loved each other. Terri was the one to break it.

"I've got something for you. Stay put." She rose and left the room.

Charity waited, curious.

In a short while her sister returned, a plastic bag hanging over one arm, two large boxes clutched against her side with the other.

"What's this?" Charity asked.

"For the dance tonight. You've been so busy writing, I was afraid you wouldn't have anything to wear."

She could have protested. She had a walk-in closet full of great clothes at home. But she hadn't thought about the dance when she'd returned to Kings Meadow with Terri this afternoon. It had been the very last thought on her mind.

"Go on," Terri urged. "Open them."

Charity opened the lid of the first box. Inside was a pink straw hat with a sparkly band around the crown. She cocked a brow in her sister's direction.

"Pink's your favorite color," Terri said, excitement in her eyes. "Now the other box."

Charity obeyed, and a soft gasp escaped her lips when she saw what was inside—the prettiest pair of cowgirl boots she'd ever seen. They were pink with pale-brown accents. Dancing boots, if ever she'd seen any.

Terri pulled the box off her lap and pointed at the plastic bag.

The dress inside the bag was the same shade of pink as the hat and boots. It had spaghetti straps and an empire waist with a free, flowing skirt. Like the boots, it had been made for dancing.

"Let's get ready," Terri said. "The dance starts in an hour."

Charity looked toward the clock on the nightstand. Had she been up here alone for that long? "Maybe I shouldn't go. I don't have any makeup on and—"

"You're going, sis. This is the first night of a better life. You'll see."

Another protest rose in her throat, but she swallowed it back. She didn't have to hide away. Not from the people of Kings Meadow. Not from anyone in her past or her future.

She wasn't afraid anymore.

When Buck entered the high school gymna-sium—sparkling and glimmering decorations everywhere—a live band was playing soft instrumental music from the stage on the far side of the room. His gaze swept over the crowd, looking for one particular person. He didn't see her.

He'd kept his promise. He'd spent the hours since she walked out of his house making sure he knew exactly how he felt and what he wanted. And when it came right down to it, nothing she'd said had changed how he felt. He loved her. End of story.

All I have to do is make her believe it.

Several people greeted him as he moved deeper into the gym. Folks who hadn't seen each other for years, even decades, talked to one another, many wearing animated expressions.

Buck nodded, said quick hellos, but didn't allow himself to be waylaid. He wanted—needed—to find Charity. He searched for her first along the east side of the gym before crossing the floor near the stage and starting down the west side. He was halfway back to the doors when Charity stepped into view, followed by her sister and brother-in-law.

She looked amazing. Bright. Fully alive. She should wear that color all the time if it did that for her.

He set off in her direction. She didn't see him right away as she talked to Edna Franklin, a history teacher at Kings Meadow High. But then she glanced up and grew still, her gaze never wavering as he closed the last distance between them.

"Hey, Charity." From the corner of his eye, he saw Terri and Rick move away. He sensed it was a kindness and not because they didn't want to speak to him.

"Hey, Buck."

He touched his hat brim as he looked at the teacher. "Evenin', Mrs. Franklin."

The older woman smiled. "Good evening, Buck." After a quick glance back and forth between her two former students, she excused herself.

Buck hardly noticed the teacher's departure. His attention was back on the vision in pink. "You came. I wasn't sure you would."

"No more hiding. I'm done with that."

It wasn't the pretty color she wore that had made the difference. He saw that now. Something was different on the inside of her.

The band started playing a Lady Antebellum song. A country waltz. A love song.

"Care to dance, Miss Anderson?"

She looked up at him for the longest while without answering. Would she refuse? Had he hoped for too much? But at last, she offered him her hand. He took it and led her to the dance floor.

THE MELODY COULD BARELY BE HEARD ABOVE THE beating of Charity's heart as Buck placed his hand on the small of her back. Before he could clasp her right hand in his left, she whipped off her hat and let it dangle from her fingertips against his back. Then they began to turn and flow and slide.

For a long while, she rested her forehead near his collarbone. But then she looked up and found him watching her, and it seemed her heart stopped beating for several seconds. She stumbled, but he didn't let her lose her balance.

It would be like that, always, if she let him love her. He wouldn't let her lose her balance. That's the kind of man he was. He would make certain they kept time to the same music.

So this is what it feels like.

To be loved.

To be cherished.

And to love and cherish in return.

She would have to make a few tweaks to the book that was nearly finished. The words she'd written hadn't captured this emotion that welled inside of her. How could she have described how it felt when she'd never experienced it until now?

Buck smiled, and a slow burn began inside of her chest. He mouthed the words of the lyrics, and she tingled all the way down to her toes.

No, she definitely hadn't known about this. About the way a crowd could fade entirely away, leaving only this man and the melody. About the desire to laugh and cry at the same time. About—

The music didn't stop, but Buck did. He released her from his embrace. But it wasn't long until his hands gently cupped the sides of her face. And there, in front of a gymnasium full of friends and strangers, Buck kissed her. A kiss that made her weak in the knees, completely breathless, and every other cliché she'd ever read or written.

When he ended the kiss, he didn't draw away. He pressed his forehead against hers and said, "In case you're wondering, Charity, I plan on kissing you a lot. For the rest of my life if you'll let me. Because I can't imagine living even a single minute without you."

Perhaps she had been a little afraid when she'd come here tonight. Not of who she might see or of what she might remember. No, she'd been afraid of never hearing him say those words.

"I love you, Charity."

And those words.

They were writing a brand-new story now, she and Buck, starting tonight. And like every good romance novel, the happily-ever-after ending was guaranteed.

Reading Group Guide

1. Charity kept a painful secret all to herself for many years. In what ways was she adversely affected because of her silence?

2. Buck gave up his own dreams to care for his parents and to help his older brother finish college and get his Master's Degree. Now it is hard for Buck to accept help in return. Is it easier for you to give help than receive it? If so, why?

3. Charity finds a sense of healing with her dog and Buck's horses. Have animals ever been a source of comfort for you?

4. Charity realizes that sin, even when forgiven, has consequences that can linger. Has that been true in your life? How did you move forward in victory in those situations?

5. Charity and Buck both tried to protect themselves from future hurt by keeping others at arm's length. Have you ever done the same? Did it work?

6. Charity came to believe—without realizing it at first—that God wouldn't want her to be happy because of her sinful actions/feelings. Have you ever viewed God that way? How do you avoid misunderstanding the invisible God?

7. Charity and Buck have older siblings who speak wisdom into their lives. Do you have a family member or friend who does the same for you?

8. Do you have a favorite character from *Whenever You Come Around*? Who is it and why?

9. There comes a moment when Charity realizes that Buck sees the "real" Charity. Everyone wants to be seen, to know their lives matter to someone. Have you experienced the love of Elroi, the God who sees (Gen 16:13)? If not, I encourage you to look to Him today. He sees you, and you matter to Him.

A Letter from the Author

I hope you enjoyed returning once again to Kings Meadow in *Whenever You Come Around*. I have had so much fun spending time in this very special community. With each story, I treasure my "friendship" with these characters more and more.

When the idea for *Whenever You Come Around* first starting rolling around in my head, it was a very different story from the novel you are holding in your hands. It's one of the things I love so much about being a novelist. As I write, I get to see both the characters and plot change and mature until I finally type "The End".

Next up is my novella in the Year of Weddings novella series, *I Hope You Dance*. It will release as an e-book in July 2015 and will be in print with the two other summer novellas at a later date. *I Hope You Dance* is set in Kings Meadow in the weeks leading up to a big wedding (not telling whose, but I bet you can guess). Readers briefly met the hero and heroine in *Whenever You Come Around*. Skye Foster, dance instructor, and Grant Nichols, a man with two left feet, have to be all wrong for each other. Right?

As I write this note to readers, two new characters with hurts and hang-ups of their own are braving a cold and snowy December in Kings Meadow. Maybe love can warm their hearts. Look for *Keeper of the Stars* in early 2016.

I look forward to hearing from my readers on Facebook (http://facebook.com/robinleehatcher) and on my website and blog (http://www.robinleehatcher.com), so I hope you'll drop by. Until next time . . .

In the grip of His grace,
Robin

About the Author

ROBIN LEE HATCHER IS THE BESTSELLING AUTHOR of over seventy books. Her well-drawn characters and heart-warming stories of faith, courage, and love have earned her both critical acclaim and the devotion of readers. Her numerous awards include the Christy Award for Excellence in Christian Fiction, the RITA® Award for Best Inspirational Romance, Romantic Times Career Achievement Awards for Americana Romance and for Inspirational Fiction, the Carol Award, the 2011 Idahope Writer of the Year, and Lifetime Achievement Awards from both Romance Writers of America (2001) and American Christian Fiction Writers (2014). *Catching Katie* was named one of the Best Books of 2004 by the Library Journal.

Robin began her writing career in the general market writing mass market romances for Leisure Books, HarperPaperbacks, Avon Books, and Silhouette. In 1997, after several years of heart preparation, Robin accepted God's call to write stories of faith and hasn't looked back since. She has written both contemporary and historical women's fiction and romance for HarperCollins Christian Fiction (Thomas Nelson and Zondervan), Revell, Steeple Hill, Tyndale House, Multnomah, and WaterBrook.

Robin enjoys being with her family, spending time in the beautiful Idaho outdoors, reading books that make her cry, and watching romantic movies. Robin and her husband make their home on the outskirts of Boise, sharing it with Poppet the high-maintenance Papillon, and Princess Pinky, the DC (demon cat).